BEAUTIFULLY HEALED

CANDIED CRUSH #19

CHARITY PARKERSON

—Warning: This book is intended for readers over the age of 18.

INTRODUCTION

Baker's heart has been broken way too many times for him to believe in love. Seth has no plans to disabuse him of that notion. They're both idiots.

All of Baker's adult life has been spent building a respected and successful law firm. The few times he's taken attention away long enough to focus on love, it's always ended the worst way possible. He doesn't believe in happy endings or even good people. That's why he can't understand why he can't shake Seth.

Seth and Baker had some fun once. That's all it was to either of them. Seth believes in science.

Chemical attraction. That's all. He's just as baffled as Baker as to why he keeps seeing Baker every time he closes his eyes. That probably means he should stay away.

When they find themselves thrust together again, one of them will have to start believing in more than chemistry. Otherwise, they'll never be healed from the past that shaped them.

ONE

WITH HIS FACE buried in his pillow, Baker fought not to moan his name. Baker flattened his palms against the mattress and pushed. He stared down the line of his body, harshly reminding himself that the ass he fucked was fake. It was only silicone and lube, tricking his brain into thinking of Seth. Baker needed to remember Seth wasn't there. He never would be.

He watched his glistening cock saw in and out of the masturbation toy. Aggravation clawed at his brain even as the pressure built, and his balls drew up tight. Baker buried his face again. With his eyes squeezed closed, Baker saw him. Sweat-soaked tanned skin. Perfect blond hair made even lighter by

1

the sun. Blue eyes. Perfect. A cry gathered in Baker's throat as he recalled the way Seth clasped the sheets, holding on while Baker fucked him. Seth's moans still filled Baker's head the same way Baker filled the fake ass with cum. Baker bit the pillow. He would not cry Seth's name. The orgasm brought him back to reality. It wasn't the same. When Baker had been inside Seth, his explosion had stolen a piece of him. Baker had shaken and gasped, devastated by his discovery. He wanted more than one night. Baker hadn't gotten it.

Seth didn't call or act as if anything had happened at all. Baker angrily cleaned up the mess he had made. Seth Black was the physician to the stars. He only made house calls to the richest of the rich and was always in high demand. Baker knew Seth's busy career wasn't why he hadn't called. They had been a one-night stand. At the thought, Baker sat on the edge of the bed and stared at nothing. He should let it go. Seth was Baker's doctor. They would see each other again, eventually. It would be awkward if Baker canceled his next checkup.

. . .

Baker glimpsed his reflection in the mirror above his dresser. In three months, he would be forty-one. There were a few gray hairs making themselves known at his temples. He had started asking his stylist to rid him of them at each appointment, but he knew they were there. There was no stopping the hands of time. It was just another reminder he should look for someone who was actually interested in him. Seth was no more than a fantasy now.

"Maybe I could get your heart pumping a little faster."

Seth's words wouldn't leave Baker's head. They had seen each other at a nightclub and had one night. That was it. It had been six weeks. They wouldn't be seeing each other naked again. Baker wasn't a fool. He knew how the world worked. Seth knew his worth, and that worth would buy him all the men half his age. Baker shouldn't be bitter. The problem was those gray hairs. Baker had thought his life would be different by now. His chest tightened. He tried rubbing away the sudden sharp pain. It was like his body had to remind him at the worst possible time he was getting older by giving him indigestion. He needed to get moving anyhow. Baker had promised to take his assistant to lunch at his country club. Aric was also Baker's friend, and it was his birthday. Baker had tried giving Aric the day off, but Aric was too loyal. He claimed his position with Baker didn't feel like work. Sometimes, Baker wished he had met Aric sooner—like before Aric had found his husband and Baker had ruined himself for all others with Seth. Aric and he had a lot in common. They always had something to talk about. Aric was a more comfortable choice for Baker. Baker had to settle for friendship now. As he always did with everyone.

With that depressing thought at the forefront of his mind, Baker pushed to his feet and headed for the shower. He couldn't be late for another day of pretending life was perfect. Otherwise, what would his one and only friend think?

The rhythmic sound of feet slapping the treadmill combined with the sound of Seth's heartbeat pounding in his ears. He ran faster, trying to match the beat. Too late, it occurred to him he could hear everything so acutely over his usual playlist because a migraine was on its way. By the time Seth killed the treadmill, he squinted against the light, and the smell of the disinfectant used to clean the equipment had him gagging. It was obvious his cleaning crew had disinfected his home gym recently.

Damn. He hated days like today. Seth had no choice but to keep going. He had a full list of patients to see today. Unlike most doctors, Seth couldn't sit in his office between visits and rest. Seth was a celebrity doctor. He spent his days driving from massive estate to massive estate, treating patients who couldn't freely walk into a regular doctor's office. To most, his job might sound like the perfect career. In truth, it was mostly hell. A lot of his patients expected he would freely write them opioid prescriptions for nothing. After all, they paid him big bucks to be at their bidding. If he wanted to keep his license, life didn't work that way. His job was like wrangling spoiled toddlers. He dealt with people all day long who believed they could buy anything and anyone. Seth and his integrity weren't for sale. His only saving grace was that he had been practicing for long enough he had a loyal client list. Most of them had already realized Seth wouldn't take their shit or be their dealer. Still, the occasional diva slipped through. He didn't know if he had it in him today.

Seth swallowed hard several times through taking a shower. He had a bad feeling this headache would be one of those breakthrough ones that sidetracked his day. Seth had found a combination of medications that worked for him a long time ago, but still there were days he couldn't get out of bed. He couldn't afford for that to happen today. There was too much to do. His body didn't give a shit what he could afford.

With his eyes squeezed shut, Seth pressed his forehead against the cool shower wall. He tried to go somewhere else in his mind while he forced his muscles to relax. Air filled his lungs as he concentrated on breathing. Sometimes meditation worked wonders. He tried clearing his mind. An image flared to life in his head of Baker gripping his sheets. Seth gasped. The sound reverberated from the walls, accosting his overly sensitive ears.

He wasn't sure why he hadn't been able to forget Baker or their night together. Seth had a nonstop flow of men who chased him. Mostly they were younger guys who wanted to snag a doctor, but Seth wasn't one to complain. Baker was closer to Seth's age. He was also the first person Seth had approached first in years. Seth had gone to a popular night club after agreeing to meet some twenty-something for a drink. The guy had shown up high on something. Seth had ditched him within five minutes of arrival. Then he had spotted Baker. Baker was one of Seth's patients. It had been unprofessional as hell for Seth to ask Baker to dance. That hadn't stopped Seth from crossing every line. He regretted nothing.

Seth's muscles relaxed. His headache ebbed. He drew a steadying breath. With his eyes closed, Seth held on to the image of Baker in his mind and finished his shower. He had gotten good at blindly doing mundane tasks over the years. As long as the pain continued to lessen, he could deal with not seeing. Baker kept him company in his mind. His dark blue eyes were gorgeous. Baker looked as expensive and intelligent as he was. He terrified Seth because he was Seth's equal. Baker wasn't some guy half Seth's age, looking for a sugar daddy. He knew his worth and wouldn't tolerate any bullshit. Baker would take a one-night stand and never call, because he didn't need Seth for anything other than release. The guy had been damn good in bed and Seth couldn't go back for seconds. With someone like Baker, twice was a relationship. No one played a guy like Baker. He was too cunning and mature for a dalliance. Baker Cox was a prize. Seth needed to forget him.

Seth stumbled from the shower and hovered over the toilet. For a moment, he genuinely believed he would lose his breakfast. He drew a few steadying breaths.

"You've had two appointments cancel this morning and one reschedule. Would you like me to call a few of your afternoon appointments and see if they would like to have their appointments moved up?"

. . .

Seth didn't bother opening his eyes or covering his nudity. Kye had been working for Seth for twelve years, since Kye was eighteen, to be exact. Kye had started as a lab courier for Seth before moving up to also being his assistant. With Seth's backing and long hours on Kye's part, Kye was now Seth's NP slash assistant. After so many years of being underneath each other's feet, they had zero boundaries. Seth wouldn't have it any other way.

When Seth didn't respond, Kye quickly and correctly assessed the situation. "I'll grab your meds and cancel your eleven thirty. After you get a couple of hours of rest, you can let me know if I need to clear this afternoon's schedule."

"Thanks, Kye." Even to Seth's ears, his words sounded ragged. He stumbled through the bathroom and into his bedroom before falling into bed nude and wet. His bedroom was pitch dark, even though it was close to nine in the morning. That was also thanks to Kye. It was obvious Kye had immediately gone into action, pulling the blackout drapes and turning off all the lights. A sigh of relief escaped Seth as his muscles relaxed a hair. He tried to stay awake, anticipating Kye's return with a drink and his meds. Time ticked by with no sign of Kye. By the time his bedroom door opened, Seth was ready to skip the meds in lieu of sleep. Then Seth's bed dipped at his hip. Seth's gaze moved that way. Only the barest of light from the hallway showed Kye's small form next to him. His brown hair had a bit of a halo from Seth's headache blurring his vision.

Kye set his hand on Seth's chest.

Seth's heart skipped a beat. There was something wrong.

"Chrissy's nurse just called."

Seth's heart stopped beating for half a second before taking a dive. He knew without hearing the rest. His sister was gone.

TWO

THE POPULAR LUNCHEON spot in downtown L.A. was nowhere near as busy as Baker feared it would be. It was mid-week, but still. Lately, it didn't seem to matter what day he went anywhere. Everything was always packed. Aric looked genuinely pleased with his boutique gift card and bonus check. As much as Baker made it out to be part of Aric's gift, Aric earned it. He put up with a lot from Baker. The sad part was Aric's life had been so hard, he didn't even recognize how hard he worked for Baker. Baker saw it, though. He would always take care of Aric.

"Do you feel a year older?"

. . .

A bright smile lit Aric's face. His gorgeous amber eyes flashed with good humor. "Truthfully, I feel a year younger. Everything has been going so great lately. It's like years have been lifted from me. I kind of hate that I said that. Hopefully, I didn't just jinx my life."

Baker snorted. Aric's husband, Enzo, thought Aric hung the moon. At one point, Baker hadn't been so sure of their relationship, but Enzo loved Aric more than anything. That was all Baker wanted for Aric. "Please. That husband of yours worships the ground you walk on. He'd likely physically fight a jinx to keep you happy."

Aric blushed. He opened his mouth, as if to respond, but Baker's phone rang, cutting him off.

Baker pulled an apologetic face. He wished he could shut off his phone for Aric. With his job, that wasn't an option. Seth's name was on the face of his device.

He tried not to look as desperate as he felt as he answered. "Hello?"

"Baker, it's Seth." Fuck. His voice was all groggy—like it had been the morning Baker left his bed. "I need you."

God help him. Baker's cock stirred. "You have me. Just tell me when and where."

"Chrissy passed away."

Baker's heart dropped. He set his napkin on the table. Aric read his expression and motioned for the check. "I'll head to the office and get started on honoring Chrissy's final wishes. Whenever you're ready to meet there, I'll be waiting."

"I know it's asking a lot, but do you mind coming here? I'm stuck in bed with a migraine. As much as my mind thinks I can power through for Chrissy, my body isn't having it."

Baker couldn't move fast enough to get to Seth. "Of course. Give me an hour."

"Thank you, Baker. I really appreciate it."

Baker watched Aric taking care of everything, as always and even though it was supposed to be his birthday. His mind froze for a second. He was blessed beyond words to have Aric. For once, Baker wanted to be that person for someone else. He didn't know if rushing away from Aric's birthday celebration was the right choice.

"Don't even think about me," Aric said quietly, as if reading his mind.

. . .

Baker's mind unfroze. "It's no inconvenience," he said into the phone, unsure of how to end the first conversation he'd had with Seth in weeks.

For a moment, Seth didn't respond. They listened to each other breathe. "I'll see you soon."

The call disconnected and Baker was slow to put it away. He wanted to cling to the few moments he had Seth's attention again before coming back to reality. Aric already had their food boxed up, paid for, and was gathering their things.

Baker shook himself from his shock. "Apologies for cutting your birthday lunch short. Chrissy Black passed this morning."

Aric's expression fell. "Oh, no. Don't worry about me. This is more important. I hate that she's gone. Obviously, she's been sick a long time, and it was only a matter of time, but still. She was so nice."

. . .

Baker nodded along as they headed for the car. He had been the Black family's solicitor since he had started his practice. Baker had settled the affairs of Seth and Chrissy's father ten years ago. Then Chrissy had been injured in an equestrian accident that had left her bedridden five years ago. She had been slowly deteriorating ever since. Baker stopped by once a week to visit. At first, it had been business. It had taken several visits for Chrissy to feel up to making it through her end-of-life planning. Over the course of his visits, Chrissy had charmed him. Even in her terrible state, she found humor in everything. Her death was a true loss to the world. He didn't doubt Seth was devastated.

Since it was Aric's birthday, Baker had driven his personal car. Normally, Aric drove them everywhere in the company vehicle. Aric being Aric, he plucked the keys from Baker's pocket and took charge. Baker slid into the passenger seat without argument. His mind was a bit of a mess. It was likely for the best he didn't drive. His mind raced on autopilot while Aric drove. The car stopped and Aric disappeared before reappearing. Baker blinked as Aric passed him Chrissy's file. Then they were off again.

. . .

Aric spoke while he drove. "I told Sandra to clear your afternoon schedule. Joshua said he would handle your morning court appearances." They pulled into Seth's driveway. "I'll call Enzo to come get me, so you'll have your car. If you need more time off past tomorrow, just let me know. I'll make sure everything gets moved around."

The lump in Baker's throat grew larger. "You deserved a better birthday than this. I don't make you feel appreciated enough."

With the car parked, Aric leaned Baker's way and kissed his cheek. "You may be my boss, but you're also my friend. So it's doubly my job to take care of you. Don't worry about me. Spending the rest of the day with my husband is no hardship."

Baker knew everything Aric said was true, but his guilt didn't ease. They were friends first, as far as Baker was concerned. He didn't think he was ever as good of a friend to Aric as Aric was to him. "Still, I'm sorry. I'd hoped for a different day."

Aric waved off his concerns and grabbed his box of food. "Don't worry about me at all. I plan to sit here and finish my lunch while I wait for Enzo. You know I'm perfectly capable of keeping my own company."

Baker knew that, and that was why he hated it so much. "Happy birthday, love."

Aric flashed him a smile and waved him away.

With a deep breath to steady himself, Baker stepped from the car and headed for the door. The last time he had been here, there had been a world of different circumstances. His stomach had shaken with anticipation. Now dread built. Despite being a professional used to dealing with high-stress situations, Baker hadn't expected to face Seth today. It was completely selfish for him to think about the last time they had been together. He couldn't help it.

Seth was in his head. Baker rang the doorbell with his heart in his throat.

While he waited, Baker eyed Seth's house to give his mind something else to do other than panicking. Seth's house was gorgeous. It was a cream-colored stone with the ocean as a backdrop. The place was huge and perfectly landscaped with tropical flowers and palm trees. He knew from previous visits the front portion of his house was Seth's home office. He had a nurse practitioner who ran his life much like Aric did for Baker. Baker had only met Kye once in passing. The guy was always too busy accepting deliveries, seeing patients, keeping files and supplies in order, and catching minor issues that cropped up throughout the day. Baker knew Seth couldn't live without Kye any more than Baker could live without Aric. Too bad Kye was a bitch.

The door opened and Kye eyed Baker from head to toe with open contempt in his hazel eyes. "I would've come to get Chrissy's file. There's no reason for you to be here."

.   .   .

Baker barely suppressed an eye twitch as he stepped inside without invitation. "Actually, no. You couldn't have. I cannot legally pass private information to you. The law doesn't work that way. It has to be me, and only me, who handles Chrissy's final wishes."

Kye headed toward his office while Baker still spoke, as if already bored by him. "He's in his bedroom. I'm aware you already know how to find that." There was no missing the cattiness in Kye's tone.

Thankfully, the tiny brunette had already dismissed him, saving Baker some embarrassment. Still, Baker pinched the spot between his eyes before heading down the hall. Seth's house screamed old money. In fact, that was how Baker had ended up as the Black family attorney. Even though Baker was born in England, and his family still lived in West Sussex, he too came from old money. It seemed no matter where he went, old money found old money like a magnet. The Black family wouldn't trust their assets with just any solicitor. It had to be one of their own. Tradition never died.

· · ·

At Seth's bedroom door, Baker took another deep breath before knocking. He waited for Seth's groggy-sounding "come in" before heading inside. The room was plunged into inky darkness. If he hadn't been in Seth's bed once already, he wouldn't have known how to find it. The scent of Seth's cologne overcame him, transporting Baker to a different time. His eyes automatically fell closed. He caught himself inhaling, wanting more. A knot formed in his stomach. He swallowed. Sometimes Baker feared he would never stop wanting Seth. His desire was like a sickness. Baker couldn't control it. Seth was a drug. Baker wanted to taste him again.

"Baker?"

Baker's soul cried out as he heard his name on Seth's lips in the dark. He had to force his eyes open. He wasn't here for himself. "I'm here." As the words left his lips, Baker recognized how deeply he meant them. Seth's sister and best friend was gone. Baker couldn't be anywhere else.

He was here. Seth felt numb all the way to his core, but something stirred inside him at the sound of Baker's voice in the dark. It felt a lot like comfort. He knew Baker would take charge and ease him.

"If you want, you can turn the bathroom light on so you're not stumbling around in the dark." Seth would offer to let Baker turn on the bedroom light, but his brain couldn't take it.

The bathroom light flared to life, casting a soft glow into the bedroom. Seth quickly turned away like a vampire being scalded by sunlight. Baker still didn't make a sound. He chanced a peek. Baker moved around the bedroom, setting a file on the dresser. As Seth looked on, Baker sent a text and emptied his pockets on top of the file. Seth's eyelids grew heavy, as if his body understood everything would be taken care of while he rested. Time slipped away. The bed dipped beside him, pulling him from his sleep and making him realize he had drifted off. The room was pitch black again, but Seth's heart knew it was Baker climbing into bed next to him.

· · ·

Baker made a shushing sound as he wrapped Seth in his embrace. "Go to sleep."

Seth's muscles relaxed in Baker's hold. The world disappeared. Everything would still be there in a few hours. For now, he was exactly where he needed to be. They both knew this was the real reason he had called Baker. His head hurt too bad to deny it now.

THREE

THE SCENT of freshly brewed coffee pulled Seth from a deep sleep. With his head clear, he could finally focus on his surroundings. He caught a glimpse of Kye slipping from the room after leaving a tray of coffee and meds behind. His gaze slid to the man sleeping inches away. The light from the bathroom highlighted his features, giving Seth the freedom to watch him sleep. Baker was that guy. The one who always showed up. That was likely why everyone always took advantage of him. In the courtroom, Baker was a shark. The rest of the world ran roughshod over him. That included Seth.

. . .

Seth's gaze dropped to Baker's sexy mouth. He had traced those lips with his crown right before Baker had sucked his dick. There was a small part of his brain that recognized Seth focused on anything and everything to keep from facing reality. He shied away from the truth that waited to body slam him back into the present. For a few moments longer, Seth wanted to hang on to the night he had spent with Baker. That had been the last time Seth could recall being happy. How odd.

There was no such thing as love. Not really. Love was a chemical reaction. Attraction was just pathways in the brain, mistaking another human as a reward. All the scientific knowledge in the world didn't save Seth as he stared at Baker. He wanted seconds.

Without realizing what he had done, Seth's fingertips traced Baker's lips. Beneath his touch, Baker's lips parted on a soft pant. Baker's eyes opened. Their gazes met. Seth didn't hesitate to replace his fingers with his mouth. Baker didn't deny him. He absorbed Seth's fury without complaint.

. . .

Seth kept moving until he had Baker rolled beneath him. It wasn't until their bodies met Seth recalled his nudity. As far as he was concerned, that meant fewer clothes standing between them. He moved from Baker's mouth to his neck. When his lips touched Baker's throat, Baker's arms encircled him. The first pain hit, seizing Seth's heart. A stuttered breath escaped him and Baker's hold tightened. Then the shaking hit. His sister was gone. He would never hear her laugh or see her smile again. Seth was alone. As the tears hit, Seth stayed hidden in the crook of Baker's neck. Baker held him and stroked his back while the worst passed.

For much longer than necessary, Seth let Baker soothe him. When he couldn't drag it out any longer, he rolled from the bed without looking back. "I'm sorry."

"You have nothing to be sorry about."

. . .

Seth slipped inside the bathroom and washed his face. He avoided his reflection while he found a pair of shorts. By the time he returned to the bedroom, Baker was up and making calls. Seth sipped his coffee and downed his meds while lost in his head. His gaze slid Baker's way. Baker's clothes were wrinkled, and his hair was a mess, but he somehow still looked unruffled. If Seth hadn't fallen apart, he could straddle Baker's hips right now. He wished his heart would let him get back to it. Seth didn't like the way he felt.

Baker disconnected his call. "Aric called all of your extended family and spoke with a transport service. As you know, Chrissy wished to be cremated and asked that no funeral be held. She said no family members except you really gave a damn about her and she didn't want those—and I'm quoting here— those no-good bastards pretending to cry over her ashes, hoping she left some money for them."

A chuckle slipped from Seth without his permission. Despite Baker's British accent, he could hear Chrissy saying that. "That sounds like her."

. . .

Baker's smile slipped away. He set his hand on the file lying on the dressing. "This is Chrissy's will. Besides a few small bequeaths to staff members, she's left everything to you. The moment she passed, everything moved to trusts, so the staff and bills will be paid until you're ready to go through each item and decide what you want to do. I'm on top of everything, so there's no rush. Just tell me when you're ready to proceed."

Even though they had known Chrissy wouldn't likely live to see the end of the year, Seth still felt an ounce of rage toward the unfairness of life. Chrissy had set all her affairs in order, planning every detail of her death, so he wouldn't have to worry about it. Now he felt useless.

"It's odd. Everything is so handled. It's like I'm not needed at all. I can go back to work and everyone can just act like she never existed without even a funeral to mark her passing."

. . .

Baker moved to a chair near the window and sat. "That's not necessarily true. I'm sure you don't have a need for two homes, and that will need to be sorted, but I get what you're saying. I also think that was the point."

At Baker's claim, Seth's gaze shot to him.

A kind smile touched Baker's lips as he explained. "I spent a great deal of time with Chrissy. She very much felt like a burden to everyone. It's my opinion she wanted you to treat her death as a footnote. Since her accident, she felt like she stole too much time from you. She wanted you to be free of her and she wanted to control what she could. That meant no funeral, no fake crying, and no fighting over her things."

"That sounds like her."

At Seth's claim, Baker held his stare. "She loved you very much."

. . .

Seth's throat swelled, and it hit him. Baker was a bigger part of his life than he had recognized. The night he had taken Baker home, he had known he could, because it was Baker. Baker had always been around, hanging in the background of Seth's life.

"I should've called."

Baker blinked as if confused by Seth's sudden claim. "Surely there was nothing you could've said that you haven't said a thousand times. Chrissy knew you loved her."

Seth shook his head. "You. I should've called you after our night together."

Baker looked away and stood. It was obvious his change in topic made Baker uncomfortable. "I'll leave Chrissy's will with you. It's your copy. You can go over it at your leisure."

. . .

At Baker's avoidance, Seth realized the truth. He had hurt Baker by not calling. "Will you go with me to Chrissy's tomorrow? I don't know if I'm ready to actually do anything with her things yet, but I also need to go."

At his question, Baker met his gaze again. "I can do that."

Seth felt driven to say something. He didn't know what exactly, but he needed Baker to know he hadn't been just a one-night stand. "Baker, I—"

"Seth, your aunt is on the phone and there's no convincing her you're too busy to talk."

A shot of aggravation ran through Seth at Kye's interruption. "Just hang up on her, fuck. I'm nowhere near ready to deal with this bullshit."

. . .

Baker stood. "I'll take the call. You shouldn't have to deal with this yet."

Kye's hackles visibly rose. "I can take care of it. I don't need your help."

At the spitefulness in Kye's tone, Baker held his hands up in surrender. "I'm sure you're more than capable. I was just trying to—"

Kye closed the door with a snap halfway through Baker's explanation, cutting him off.

Baker's gaze slid Seth's way. Humor flashed in his eyes. "I don't think he likes me very much."

Seth sidled closer, incapable of resisting Baker's sexiness. "It's not you. Kye doesn't like anyone." His hands slid across Baker's hips without permission from his brain. "If it makes you feel any better, I like you."

.   .   .

Baker's gaze moved over Seth's face, as if searching for the truth. His expression gave nothing away. "I like you too. You should get some rest. I'll come back in the morning."

"Or you could stay the night."

Baker took a breath as if he started to say something, but then a small smile touched his lips. "I'll see you in the morning."

With a nod, Seth took a step back. Baker had always been a little difficult to read. He could have chosen to deny Seth because it was a bad time or because Seth hadn't called last time. There was no way for Seth to tell. He could only take his loss with grace.

"Be careful going home."

.   .   .

With a dip of his chin, Baker gathered his things and headed for the door. Seth watched with his heart in his throat as Baker put on his shoes. Before Baker slipped from the room, he glanced over his shoulder. Their gazes met one final time. Seth had to take a breath. He would be alone again soon. It was his fault.

Baker barely made it from Seth's room with his heart intact. Truthfully, he had always known he was more than a little attracted to Seth. The night he had gone home with Seth—for Baker—it had been a long time coming. Unfortunately, Baker thought it might have also been a mistake. Things were kind of blurry now. Seth wasn't the type to settle down. Nothing good could come of them falling into bed together again.

As Baker headed for the door, a movement from the corner of his eye caught Baker's attention. The light was still on inside Kye's office, even though it was ten at night. He could see Kye hunched over his desk, typing notes into his laptop. Baker headed that way, even though he knew only venom awaited him.

. . .

"You're still here."

Kye glanced up. There was a deep line between his hazel eyes. "Some of us work for a living."

Baker nodded. "I'm aware. Can I get you anything before I leave? Coffee? Hard drugs?"

To Baker's surprise, Kye's mouth lifted in one corner in a half smile. Baker imagined that was the closest he had ever come to pulling any smile from Kye.

"I'm good. Be careful going home."

With a nod, Baker backed away before Kye turned feral again. He didn't imagine Kye would ever like him. Baker wasn't usually bothered by that. Lawyers weren't normally liked. It wasn't his job to win a popularity contest. Baker's place was in front of his clients, protecting them. In this case, though, Kye wasn't his client or his opponent. He wasn't sure why Kye had such hatred for him, but Baker didn't like it. It was obvious Kye was an extremely loyal and hard worker. He was always in the background of Seth's life, taking care of way more than he should. Baker honestly didn't think Kye's rage was jealousy driven. Most times, he didn't seem to like Seth any better than he liked Baker. Baker would figure him out. For sanity's sake, he needed the distraction.

He could have stayed for another night with Seth. Baker damn near doubled over as that thought hit him full force in the stomach. Seth had kissed him. If Seth hadn't just lost his sister, Baker would have been inside Seth again. Baker slid behind the wheel of his car and stared at nothing. Holding Seth while he slept had been like choosing to stay in Hell. His skin had been on fire while his mind was tormented by what he would never have. Baker was dumb. Always had been. He never fell for anyone available. They were either married or emotionally withdrawn. Baker never met anyone who wanted him with equal fervor. Seth was no different. While it was true Seth was single, he would always be that way. Seth was wealthy, gorgeous, and vehemently sought after, and he knew it. He would never give up the string of young twenty-somethings that begged to warm his bed. Baker was over forty and had some miles. This was a waste of his time.

Baker stared at Seth's house. He would come back tomorrow and do his job. As Seth requested, they would go to Chrissy's and start the most basic of plans to liquidate her assets. Baker would be professional and forget any ties with Seth beyond business. Every kiss and touch had been a mistake Baker wouldn't keep making. Tonight had been their last kiss.

FOUR

AFTER LYING AWAKE ALL NIGHT, Baker wasn't surprised he wasn't ready to face Seth. Since he didn't intend to go into the office today, he normally would have dressed casually. Since he needed to keep things professional with Seth, Baker wore his usual suit and tie. To further reiterate that this was merely another workday, he had Aric drive him.

"You look nice today, by the way. I would have expected you to dress down today."

.   .   .

Baker eyed Aric. He swore the guy could read his thoughts some days. "I'm still working."

Aric made a humming sound but didn't say anything else.

Baker went back to staring at the road. Aric knew him too well. He couldn't give him any bait.

After a moment, Aric seemed to lose his resolve against his nosiness. "Is that why you made me stop, so you could grab those ridiculously expensive flowers? For professional reasons?"

Baker squared his shoulders. He would not bite. "These aren't for my client."

A knowing chuckle came from Aric's side of the car. "So, Seth is being called the client now. I see."

. . .

God help him. "What do you see?"

A smile exploded across Aric's face, but he kept his eyes on the road. "Nothing. It's just that before today, everything was Seth this and Seth that. Now he's the client. Did things go that badly yesterday?"

He hated they were friends. Not really. Baker just didn't want to discuss his feelings today. "His sister died. We're here for business," Baker reminded Aric as Aric steered into Seth's driveway.

Aric killed the engine before looking Baker's way. "Do you want to talk about it before we go inside?"

There was a ton of sympathy in Aric's eyes. Baker wanted to tell him his every thought, but now wasn't the time. Still, a knot formed in his throat. "Later."

Aric nodded. "I'm holding you to that."

. . .

With a dip of his chin and a breath for courage, Baker climbed from the car. He wasn't sure what to expect today. Seth might be cold and courteous. The way he was with other people. Or he might be like he was yesterday, hot and passionate. Baker wasn't sure which version sounded like the bigger nightmare. The door stood open, so they let themselves in. A chime sounded as they stepped over the threshold, as if Kye had set the door alarm to warn him of visitors. That made Baker wonder if he sometimes saw patients here.

Kye stepped from his office. "Oh, it's you. I was expecting the lab courier."

"Apologies. I didn't see the point in knocking on an open door. These are for you." Baker held the bouquet out to Kye. He felt Aric's fingers brush the small of his back, as if showing silent approval.

Kye eyed them with open suspicion. "What's this?"

. . .

Baker shrugged. "When I left the office this morning, there was a flower cart out front. These reminded me of you."

While still looking unsure, Kye accepted the flowers. "These reminded you of me," he said, repeating Baker's claim like he didn't understand.

With a nod, Baker explained. "Lilies are vastly underappreciated flowers. They get the least attention, even though they're arguably the most beautiful. Plus, if you treat them right, they'll continue to flourish."

Kye stared at Baker without blinking. His grip tightened on the flowers.

Baker didn't give him time to respond. "Oh, I also brought you another gift." He stepped aside and motioned Aric's way. "This is my personal assistant, Aric. Since I'll be busy with Seth today and you're run ragged covering his patients, I thought you could use a hand. Aric is amazing and ready to do whatever you need."

For a moment, Kye looked between them as if unsure of how to react. Then he visibly softened. "Hey, Aric. I'm Kye."

Aric gave a small wave, looking shy. Baker knew then he had made the right decision. Kye was overworked and undervalued. He wasn't sure it was completely Seth's fault. Baker got the feeling Kye had too much pride to admit he was drowning. Aric would help dig him out. Plus, they were similar in age. He imagined they would get on smashingly.

"Just tell me where you need me, and I swear I'll make your life easier."

Kye motioned toward his office. "Thank god. Come this way."

. . .

Aric flashed Baker a smile and went with Kye. Baker watched them go with his heart in his throat. There was no avoiding Seth any longer. Before Baker could gather his strength, Seth stepped into the foyer. A black t-shirt stretched across his wide shoulders. Jeans molded to his sexy ass. His gorgeous blue gaze moved down Baker's body as he closed the distance between them.

"Do me a favor."

Baker didn't even need to think about it. "Anything."

Seth went to work unbuttoning Baker's jacket before swiping it down Baker's shoulders. "Try to look like you enjoy my company." After tossing the jacket onto a nearby chair, he worked Baker's tie loose and tossed it on top of the jacket. "You do enjoy my company, right?" he asked as he unbuttoned the top three buttons of Baker's shirt.

"You know I do." Goddamn him.

. . .

Something dark flashed in Seth's gaze. "That's good."

They held each other's stare. Baker wondered if Seth intended to kiss him. Then Seth took a step back, and the moment was over. Baker kicked himself for falling for it again. Seth's charms were dangerous. He could make a person hate themselves. Baker wondered if he wasn't already there.

"We should go."

Seth's mouth lifted in one corner. The space between them disappeared. Baker found himself in Seth's arms again. Seth's tongue invaded his mouth. His hands kneaded Baker's ass. Good sense flew out the window. As always, he let Seth wreck him. God help him. Baker didn't know how to make the longing stop. He fell every time. Even knowing Seth would never see him as more than a distraction, Baker embraced the pain.

. . .

"I'll put these in the car and drop them by your house on my way home."

Seth pulled away at Aric's interruption. Aric pulled Baker's wallet from the inside pocket of his jacket and tucked it in Baker's back pocket.

"Don't forget this." Aric backed away, blushing, as if just realizing what he had interrupted. "Don't mind me." He walked away with the jacket and tie.

Seth's sexy chuckle had Baker's gaze moving back his way. "That really is the best assistant I've ever seen."

Baker didn't miss the way Seth's eyes flashed with appreciation as his gaze followed Aric's retreat. That was what he needed. Baker took a step back. His heart hardened. "I went through Chrissy's will again after I left here last night. To refresh my memory. While she asked that a majority of her things be sold, so you could have the money and not become a hoarder, she added a caveat that you be allowed to have the final say. She worried you might have sentimental ties to something she owned she was unaware you cared about."

"I really fucked up when I didn't call you, didn't I?"

Baker took a breath and counted to five in his head before answering. "I knew who you were before I agreed to go home with you."

A deep line appeared between Seth's eyebrows. "Is that so? And who am I?"

This time, Baker didn't take those five seconds the way he should have. "The kind of man who appreciates a good assistant."

Seth's expression snapped closed. "I went through Chrissy's will last night as well. Her wishes were made clear. We should get started."

. . .

Regret washed over Baker. No good ever came of him caring about anyone. He had known they were no more than a one-night stand. It was no one's fault but his own that he wanted more. For a moment, Baker's eyes fell closed. He wished he was somewhere else, but when he opened his eyes, Seth still stood there.

"Very well."

The quicker they got started, the faster it would be over. That was the best Baker could hope for. There was nothing good for him here.

The more time Seth spent with Baker, the more he questioned his every life decision. Seth had always appreciated beautiful men. Since he was single, he saw no point in reeling himself in. Until today, he hadn't realized he'd hurt anyone. Then he had seen himself through Baker's eyes. This entire week was quickly becoming a solid kick in the ass.

. . .

As he moved through his sister's home, he wondered if anything would ever feel right again. His mind refused to grasp that Chrissy was gone. Seth kept expecting to round the corner and see her face. He knew he should pick a few sentimental items and get started on selling the rest. Seth didn't know where to start. It didn't help matters Baker was being the shining example of a professional. He had re-buttoned his shirt in the car and only spoke when spoken to. Baker followed him from room to room in silence.

"I feel like I'm snooping."

Baker nodded. "I understand. When my mum passed, I had a hard time going through my parents' things. She still had so much stuff from my grandparents, and then all of my dad's and her things. It was a nightmare."

Seth's chest hurt. "I guess I should be grateful Chrissy planned everything down to the last letter."

. . .

"She had a lot of free time."

At Baker's remark, Seth turned his way. "You spent a lot more time with her than I realized, didn't you?"

Baker's gaze slid away. "I suppose I did."

"You're amazing."

Baker's gaze slid back Seth's way. "Not really. Chrissy and I had a lot in common."

A smile snapped to Seth's lips. "Are you a huge horse lover as well?"

"No." Baker turned away and headed for an empty chair in Chrissy's bedroom. He spoke over his shoulder as he went. "We were both terribly lonely and enjoyed having someone to talk to." Baker sat and held Seth's stare without an ounce of embarrassment. "She did worry about her horses, though."

Seth didn't know if he should feel ashamed for toying with someone who longed for human contact or be enraged at Baker for saying yes. Either way, Seth was the bastard because he hadn't stopped that night and he didn't intend to stop now. "You should have dinner with me."

"No, thank you."

"Why?"

An uncomfortable-sounding chuckle fell from Baker's sexy lips at Seth's question. "Why? Maybe because your sister just died, and I don't care to be the way you make yourself feel better. Or perhaps it's because I'm your solicitor and you're my doctor. Dear lord, it sounds like beginning of a bad joke or a really awful lawsuit."

.   .   .

"So?"

Baker looked flabbergasted by Seth's flippant tone. "What do you mean, 'so'?"

Seth made a dismissive gesture. "I mean, so what. Who cares? Do you know what the top two things I treat people for in this town are?"

A line appeared between Baker's eyebrows. "I haven't the slightest clue, but I imagine it has something to do with hard drugs."

Seth shook his head. "That's the third. No. The top two things are eating disorders and depression. Everyone in this fucking town is miserable. They're all starving themselves and popping pills. No one is the least bit happy with any aspect of their lives. They have all the money and options they could want, but they just live trapped in their heads. Do you really want to live like that?"

. . .

Baker only looked more confused than he had before Seth started talking. "Of course I don't want to be miserable. That's why I said no. You already didn't call once. Why would I set myself up for that twice?"

"You didn't call either."

Baker's expression snapped closed. "Did you want me to call?"

Seth felt oddly thrown off balance by the question. It was his turn to chuckle uncomfortably. "I don't know. Maybe. I think so." The more Seth rambled, the more everything got under his skin. "Fuck. Yeah, okay? If you had called, I would've been happy to hear from you, but maybe I just don't want to be alone tonight. Goddamn. You're my friend and everything is fucked. Chrissy is gone and nothing feels right."

"Okay."

. . .

Seth had flustered himself to the point he didn't even know what they talked about any longer. "Okay, what?"

"Okay. I'll go to dinner with you."

Seth's mind and heart immediately aligned. A sense of peace washed over him. He still hurt, but Baker was here and wasn't going anywhere. At least for tonight, Seth knew he would be okay.

With Baker's agreement to keep him company, Seth turned his attention to honestly looking for things to bring home with him. "There's the obvious, I guess. Her photo albums, personal computer, and books need to be moved to my house. I'll go through the books there and donate what I don't want to the library. Our mom's paintings." He turned in a circle, trying to think. Seth wondered how he was supposed to feel and behave. Chrissy had been thrown from her horse and trampled five years ago, leaving her paralyzed from the neck down and withering away.

She had gone from being the most active person he knew to being trapped in a frozen body in the blink of an eye. It had been hell for her. Now she was free. He was broken-hearted he would never see her again. Seth was also relieved she wouldn't have to suffer any longer.

"She loved you, but she was ready to go," Baker said, as if reading his mind.

"I know."

"You're allowed to feel how you feel about that."

Seth smiled at Baker's attempts to be a good friend. "I know."

"I haven't been able to get that night out of my head."

.   .   .

At Baker's claim, Seth stopped trying to mentally inventory each room. His gaze landed on Baker. Baker looked braced for any reaction. Seth recognized Baker tried protecting himself. That wasn't necessary. They were both adults.

"It was a spectacular night. I was surprised to find you gone the next morning."

Baker didn't back down or look away. "I had a tennis match, and you looked too peaceful to disturb."

"I told Chrissy about that night."

At Seth's confession, a smile exploded across Baker's face. "She never let on that she knew."

"She was always good at keeping my secrets." A wave of sadness washed over Seth as the words left his mouth. He didn't know who he would talk to now. "Are you ready to go?"

. . .

Baker's eyes flashed with sympathy. "If you are."

He was. At the moment, he was too tempted to demand the house stay exactly as it was—like a shrine. Seth needed to find something else to do. Baker looked like an amazing alternative to grieving. He could lose himself in Baker's dark blue eyes. That seemed like the perfect plan to him.

Baker felt like the biggest idiot ever born for accepting Seth's dinner invitation. Nothing good could come of hours in Seth's company. His body ached each time their gazes met and held. Baker's mind flashed images of their night together. His soul cried out for more. There was just something about Seth, though. Baker knew without asking they would never be more than they were right now: friends who might end up in bed together. It was depressing. It was like specially ordering his personal version of hell. He couldn't stop.

. . .

They stopped by Baker's house so Baker could change. There was no sense in him pretending this day had anything to do with business any longer. After pulling on a pair of jeans and a blue t-shirt, Baker stared at himself in the full-length mirror inside his closet. Seth had admitted to wanting Baker to call.

A smile pulled at Baker's lips. Things weren't a complete loss. Maybe he wasn't a total fool. With a shake of his head, Baker headed inside his bedroom to find some socks. He needed to let himself be happy.

"You have sexy feet."

Seth's presence in Baker's bedroom and his offhand remark startled a laugh from Baker. "What an odd thing to say."

A gorgeous and unrepentant smile stretched Seth's lips. "If you knew how many disgusting feet I see a day, you wouldn't find that a strange compliment. Plus, I just happen to think everything about you is sexy."

Baker didn't want to be flattered, but he had never seen Seth with anyone else his age. It was high praise to still be considered sexy next to people half his age. "You're not so bad yourself."

Seth's expression turned heated, warming Baker's skin. "Maybe we should order dinner in bed."

Baker's mouth went dry. "I could eat in bed."

Seth shuffled a little closer. "You're very multi-talented. I'm willing to bet you can eat and fuck me at the same time."

Damn. Baker's body burned. "Do you really want to wait for the food to arrive to find out?"

· · ·

"No."

Seth overcame him in an instant. Their mouths clashed as they tore at each other's clothes, losing their shirts. All the weeks they spent ignoring each other rose to the surface. The explosive desire they felt that night and tried to ignore ever since returned in an instant. Baker walked backward toward the bed. He kissed and teased Seth, luring him along. At the edge of the mattress, Baker sat and went to work on Seth's jeans.

His body was beautiful. Baker had a terrible time focusing on stripping Seth while Seth's sexy as fuck torso was right there. Baker couldn't stop kissing the deep line running down the center of Seth's stomach. Baker played tennis to stay in shape. He didn't look like Seth. Seth worked out. His body was hard and tight. Baker's cock leaked at the memories of being inside Seth. He was about to be there again.

"There it is. That's why I can't shake you."

· · ·

Baker's gaze moved upward and collided with Seth's. Seth said he couldn't shake Baker. He hadn't heard him wrong. His heart paused, waiting for more.

Seth cupped Baker's jaw. His thumb dragged across Baker's bottom lip. "I'll freely admit I've been with a lot of men. No one has ever looked at me the way you do. You could make an addict of me." Seth leaned down and kept coming until his body covered Baker's. Their gazes never wavered. "You would let me do anything, wouldn't you?"

Baker couldn't lie. "Yes."

"I want to use your body."

A stuttered breath left Baker at Seth's confession. He wanted that too. "Then do it. I dare you."

At his taunt, Seth leaped from the bed and stripped away the rest of their clothing faster than Baker could have dreamed. Then he was back, straddling Baker's body and invading Baker's mouth. All Baker could do was take it and fight for air. When Seth pulled away again, Baker barely gasped a few precious breaths before Seth straddled his face and led his cock to Baker's mouth. Baker didn't hesitate opening. He craved the whirlwind of being caught in Seth's furious desire.

Seth's thick cock scraped the roof of Baker's mouth. Baker sucked, wanting the salty flavor of Seth's cum in his mouth.

Seth pulled away. "No. I want more."

Before Baker could recover a single clear thought, Seth turned around. He straddled Baker's head, facing the opposite direction. Baker didn't have time to think. Seth's dick was in Baker's mouth again while Seth took Baker's cock all the way down his throat. Baker lost the ability to do anything but experience the moment. Seth took no mercy.

· · ·

He fucked Baker's mouth. Baker sucked and licked, mindlessly performing while Seth blew him like a professional. He toyed with Baker's balls before using his saliva to finger Baker's asshole. Baker spread his thighs like a wanton, begging for more when Seth immediately hit the right spot. His moans were muted around the dick in his mouth. He gave Seth everything he had to give, wanting the same. His hips rolled, seeking more. Seth's throat tightened around Baker's cock. Baker saw stars. He massaged Seth's ass cheeks and balls. Baker fingered Seth's asshole and sucked Seth's dick with all the passion in his soul.

Baker's muscles slowly tensed as the pressure climbed his shaft. He didn't want this to end, but Seth played Baker's body like a master. He knew which buttons to push and how much pressure to exert. Baker didn't stand a chance of lasting long. He was determined to bring Seth along for the ride. Baker wouldn't blow alone.

He curled his tongue and toyed with Seth's crown. It was the last playful gesture. Baker went to work. He felt Seth's muscles stiffen. Satisfaction exploded through him when Seth cried out around Baker's cock. Cum hit Baker in the back of the throat. He swallowed before he choked. It became a mindless act when Seth went wild on Baker's dick. Baker squeezed Seth's ass in a bruising grip as Seth massaged Baker internally and swallowed him. Everything inside Baker seized. The world stopped turning. It was like he died, and then ecstasy struck. Baker's body shook as wave after beautiful wave flowed through him. The hot suction on his cock owned him. Baker was still shaking and floating on air like an out-of-body experience when Seth swapped positions again. His mouth covered Baker's. Baker tasted his own cum as Seth's tongue stroked his.

This kiss was slower, sweeter. The desperation had passed. Now they were just people enjoying each other. Baker didn't want it to ever stop.

"I'm not through with you," Seth promised between kisses. For now, though, he needed this. They were the calm after the storm. Their hearts raced, fiercely beating against their chests as if trying to get closer to each other. Their labored breaths slowed a little more by the second. Seth had never been more alive. He realized in that moment how much he needed exactly what Baker gave him.

It might seem a little crazy to think about his sister in that moment, but she had been so in love with life. He knew she would want this for him. She adored the idea of him being with Baker—like her two favorite people had found each other. Chrissy wanted him to live. He felt more alive with Baker than anywhere else in the world.

Seth pulled away only far enough to press his forehead against Baker's. With his eyes closed, he breathed Baker in, savoring the moment. "You're that one person I know I can count on." As Seth made the confession, his chest tightened. A shot of fear ran through him. He leaned away and held Baker's stare. "I hope you know I'm the same. You can trust me to be here whenever you need me."

. . .

Baker's expressions were always so unreadable. Seth rarely knew what Baker thought about anything unless there was lust involved. Now Baker was back to hiding his every emotion.

"I jack off with your name on my lips more than any other."

As far as distractions went, it was a damn good one. Seth forgot what they were talking about. He didn't know how his body could burn so badly for someone who just blew his mind, but it did. Seth needed more time with Baker.

"Prove it. I want to hear you screaming my name."

"Make me."

At the taunt, Seth forgot everything. They had hours and hours to kill. Tomorrow, Baker's body would ache with the memory of Seth. Seth couldn't wait to get started.

FIVE

SETH: *My whole body is sore. I didn't have to work out this morning. Thank you for everything.*

Baker: *It was my pleasure. Perhaps we can do it again soon.*

———

At least he texted. That was all Baker could tell himself when Seth didn't respond to Baker's open invitation. He promised himself he wouldn't freak or anything. Hoping to hold true to that vow, he focused on working and Aric.

. . .

Baker flipped through his notes on everything he had missed the day before. He fought the urge to check his phone for the millionth time. His foot bobbed beneath his desk. A pain sliced through his chest and he ate some more antacids.

"Oh, I forgot to tell you. I love Kye. He's so nice."

Aric's comment was the distraction Baker needed. "Really?"

Aric laughed at Baker's reaction. "Why do you sound so surprised?"

A smile exploded across Baker's face. "I don't know. As much as I imagined there was a good person beneath his prickly exterior, I guess I didn't expect you to find it so quickly."

Aric made a dismissive gesture. "Oh, he's one hundred percent pissed off at the world, but that has nothing to do with me. I was there, making his life easier. Did you know his parents moved here from Japan when Kye was in the third grade and he speaks six languages?"

That was impressive. "Bloody hell. I hope Seth appreciates that. It's no doubt extremely helpful with the diversity of patients."

Aric leaned forward. His light amber eyes flashed with a conspiratorial light. "It turns out your hottie is the worst boss on the planet. Kye stays because Seth put him through school and pays him well, but he completely takes Kye for granted. Kye says he gets to the office at six every morning, does his job there while seeing his patients and taking on half of Seth's. Often, he doesn't leave the office before ten at night. He's burnt out and considering turning in his notice."

Baker was sucked into the gossip. "I was afraid of that. When I left there the other night, it was super late, and he was still working. He looked tired. It's no wonder he always snapping everyone's heads off."

"Oh, no. That's reserved for mostly Seth and people in Seth's circle. He's crazy bitter about his hard work going unnoticed."

Baker sat back in his chair. "Huh. I wonder if there's anything I can do beyond giving him flowers. Working that much can't be good for his health."

Aric didn't respond. The silence cut through Baker's musings. He found Aric smiling at him. His adorable dimples distracted Baker. "What?"

Aric shook his head. "It's nothing. You're an amazing person. I wish you realized it."

An uncomfortable chuckle sneaked out. "What? You don't think I know my worth?"

· · ·

To his surprise, Aric's smile slipped away. "I think people like Seth will never know your worth. As long as you keep letting him suck you in, you'll never meet anyone who deserves you."

He had to stop telling Aric things. "Do you want to get some lunch?" Baker had to do something besides think or talk about Seth. He knew he had bad taste. Always had.

Even though Aric flashed him a knowing look, he stood. "Just let me know where we're headed so I can steer the car in the right direction."

Baker had to think about it. With his horrible indigestion, nothing sounded good any longer. "How about that Mediterranean place on the beach?" Maybe some grilled shrimp wouldn't be too bad.

"Sounds good to me."

. . .

Aric drove and Baker stared out the window. He knew Aric was right. As long as Baker settled for someone who never called or texted him, he would never meet anyone nice. Baker had a long history of falling for the wrong people. Years ago, he had fallen hard for a married woman. She had been in an abusive marriage and he had let her string him along for literal years. Then she had killed herself and he hadn't learned his lesson. He had thought staying single for a few years would prove he was capable of being alone. Baker didn't need anyone. The problem was, he wanted someone. He didn't understand why things were always so hard.

When they reached the restaurant, Baker fought hard to shake his melancholy. He would forget Seth. Baker had given the guy two chances. If Seth had wanted to make a go of things, he would have. It was that simple. Aric wrapped his hands around Baker's bicep, and Baker glanced his way. For the millionth time, he wished they had been meant for more than friends. Baker might not feel the passion for Aric he felt for Seth, but maybe what he needed was something closer to this. They had a beautiful friendship. He should look for that. Maybe Kye would like to go to dinner some night. It was possible his growing bitterness for Seth would be enough of a connection to find common ground with Kye. The guy was sexy. Baker could make him smile.

As they stepped inside the restaurant, Baker turned his attention to the hostess. "A table for two, please?"

"I'm allergic to everything here. We should go."

A laugh burst from Baker at Aric's ludicrous comment. "We've eaten here a hundred..." The words died on Baker's tongue as he glanced Aric's way. At a table only feet away, Seth sat with a guy no more than twenty-three. With his arm draped across the back of the guy's chair, Seth whispered against the blond's ear. The air froze in Baker's lungs. He couldn't breathe. Seth pulled away from his date, laughing. His sexy light blue gaze landed on Baker and his smile slipped away.

. . .

Baker turned away. "You're right. Everything about this place is terrible." He held his head high but stumbled on the way to the car.

Aric tightened his grip on Baker's arm. "Holy shit, Baker. Are you okay?"

Baker massaged his chest. He felt like such an idiot. "I'm fine. Do you mind just picking somewhere else to eat?" A cold sweat rolled down his back, soaking his shirt. He couldn't breathe. Baker was so exhausted. He didn't understand why he always fell for the worst people. No doubt everything Seth said to him, he also told two or three different people a day. Baker wasn't special. Fuck. He really couldn't catch his breath. Everything felt a little out of focus, as if his brain couldn't get enough oxygen to function properly. His fingers fumbled with the seatbelt before Aric finally buckled it for him. He panted, gasping for air. Life darkened around the edges. A sense of hopelessness sank in. Baker closed his eyes and tilted his head back, resting it against the seat. He heard Aric talking to him, but he couldn't make out the words. It felt like an elephant sat on his chest, squeezing the life from him. He had known Seth would hurt him, but fuck. Baker hadn't been prepared for the crushing pain. Life felt like it was slipping away. He couldn't make it stop. Then everything went black.

Their regular delivery guy had the entrance to the driveway blocked. It was just one more irritation on top of a million other things. Seth kept his rage focused on traffic and then the blocked driveway to stop himself from thinking too much about who really pissed him off the most: himself. He should have called off his lunch date with Larkin after the night he spent with Baker. Seth knew that, but then again, they weren't exclusive. He didn't know why he was so upset. That wasn't true. Seth couldn't stop seeing Baker's face. He had obviously been sucker punched. Still, and once again, they weren't exclusive. Baker didn't really have a right to be mad. The thing was, though, if the shoe had been on the other foot, Seth might have gone to jail today. Instead, he had watched Baker immediately turn to leave, as if Baker couldn't witness Seth spending time with anyone else. Goddamn it.

. . .

As Seth came through the door, he thought to come unglued over the blocked driveway. Kye was smiling for once. That thought alone stopped him. Seth didn't make anyone smile anymore. Sometimes, he wondered if he was turning into his father. He couldn't think of anything worse than becoming the philandering hypocritical ass who had given him life. Seth couldn't call him the man who raised him because nannies and boarding schools had done that. Still, blood always ruled supreme. Maybe he had cheating genes, even though he hadn't technically cheated. Goddamn it. Seth really just wanted to park his goddamn car in the garage he paid for.

He tried taking a few calming breaths. The last thing Seth wanted was to be an even bigger prick. Instead, he stood in the doorway and waited for Kye to stop flirting so he could move his car. An unexpected smile tugged at his lips as Kye reached over and squeezed the delivery guy's bicep.

. . .

"Wow. I'm impressed. These boxes are probably nothing to you. Thank you for grabbing them for me. There's no way I could've dragged them out onto the porch by myself."

The bear-sized guy's full beard did nothing to hide his blush. "It's no problem. You shouldn't risk your back on these. Anytime you need me, just let me know. I don't mind helping you."

Kye's eyes flashed with mischief. "I should get your number then. Don't you think? In case I need you."

The guy practically tripped over his feet, setting down the boxes so he could accept the pen and card Kye held out to him. "Um. Yeah. I guess so." He scratched his number on the back of one of Kye's business cards.

Before he could grab the oversized boxes again that Kye needed picked up for the day, Kye stopped him. "You should probably also take one of my cards. In case you'd like to call me some time," Kye clarified.

Seth shook his head as he watched the pair. Kye was a gorgeous guy. He was tiny with every muscle well defined. His Asian descent made his skin look perfectly tanned while his hazel eyes stopped people short. Men tripped over themselves to get to him, but Kye never dated. He could have anyone he wanted. It seemed odd to see him flirting so hard with a deliveryman.

With numbers exchanged, Seth stepped aside so the driver could pass. He looked shell-shocked, as he should. Kye was a million times out of his league.

Seth waited until the guy was gone before commenting. "Why are you teasing that poor guy?"

Kye's smile fell at Seth's question. He snatched up the guy's number and clasped it to his chest. It was as if the tiny business card was the only thing stopping him from physically fighting Seth. "Just because someone doesn't look like you doesn't mean they're unworthy of attention."

Seth drew back. He kind of wished Kye had struck him. In the twelve years he had known Kye, Kye had never slapped him with so much venom, and that was saying a lot. All Kye hit him with was attacks lately. "What's that supposed to mean?"

Kye headed for his office while ranting over his shoulder, forcing Seth to follow. "Not everyone has your Adonis' genes, Seth. Some of us are just fucking normal and we like to be noticed too. What do you think the rest of us are out here doing while you have a string of too perfect barely legal men lining up to fuck you? We're out there looking for someone nice," he said, answering his own question before Seth could formulate a thought.

"What the hell, Kye? What's going on with you lately?"

. . .

Kye's shoulders expanded and fell—like he needed a deep breath. He set the number on his desk. "I'm turning in my two-week notice."

Seth found the nearest chair and sat. "What? I don't understand."

Kye wouldn't look directly at him. "I didn't want to do this so soon after Chrissy's passing, but I think it's for the best."

"Best for who?" Seth didn't want to lose his temper, but fuck. What else would happen today? He couldn't train someone else to do Kye's job in two weeks on top of losing Chrissy. No doubt Baker would never speak to him again. Everything was falling apart, and Seth didn't know which way was up any longer.

Kye finally turned his way and sat on the edge of the desk. "It's better for everyone, but mostly it's best for me. I used to love this job and you. Now I wake up every day feeling bitter about coming here." Kye held his stare. "I hate having to see you."

The punched-in-the-gut feeling wouldn't stop. His chest hurt. Everyone was turning against him. "I don't—"

The emergency line rang, cutting off Seth's words.

Kye picked up the phone as quickly as possible. It couldn't have been more obvious he appreciated the reprieve. "Dr. Black's office."

Kye's gaze shot to Seth. He motioned for Seth to stand. "Thank you for letting us know. Dr. Black is on his way." Kye disconnected the call and ushered Seth toward the door.

Seth tried dragging his feet. "We need to talk about this, Kye. I can't lose you. Tell me what I'm doing wrong, so I can fix it."

. . .

Kye wasn't listening. "You need to go. They've just admitted Baker into Coastal General."

Seth froze. "What?"

Kye shoved Seth's medical bag into his hands with zero mercy for Seth's sanity. "He suffered a myocardial infarction. They've started nitroglycerin, oxygen, and a blood thinner. They're asking for your consultation on surgery."

For a moment, Seth stared at Kye while the words slowly penetrated his brain. Other than slightly elevated blood pressure, Baker was in perfect health. This made no sense. He couldn't be in the hospital waiting for life-saving intervention. Seth was losing everyone, and he couldn't focus.

Kye's chest rose and fell. "Fuck. Come on. I'll drive."

. . .

Seth followed Kye while stuck on autopilot. He still didn't understand. All he knew was he couldn't lose Baker. He just couldn't. If he knew nothing else, Seth knew he had to keep Baker around. He couldn't live with any other outcome.

SIX

IN HIS YEARS on the planet, Baker had been through a lot. He had seen plenty of death and accepted he would probably die alone. Baker had suffered his fair share of depression. Not once had he felt the way he did now. While trapped in bed in a trauma room, Baker stared at his vitals on the machine he had been attached to immediately. They hadn't let Aric stay with him. Until that moment, Baker hadn't realized how much he didn't want to die in the hospital with no one there to hold his hand.

Sleep came and went. Exhaustion kept towing him under. His body was weak. Maybe Baker was being dramatic, or perhaps he truly was close to death, but Baker kind of wanted to let go. There was nothing keeping him here. The only person who would miss him was Aric. Baker had recently changed his will, leaving Aric everything. Aric didn't know that, but it freed Baker to go without guilt. Aric might mourn, but he would be better off once Baker was gone.

The numbers on the machine changed, setting off an alarm. A smile tried tugging at his lips, but he was too weak for it to be more than a phantom sensation. He would just go now. There was no reason to stay. Darkness pulled him under. The relief was massive.

"Not today, sexy."

The words sounded far away, but Baker fought to open his eyes. Surely he hadn't heard Seth's voice. The audacity. Light assaulted his pupils. Baker winced against the intrusion.

. . .

"There are those gorgeous blues. How are you feeling today?"

Today? Confusion had Baker blinking. Seth hovered over him, wearing light blue scrubs that matched his eyes and a white doctor's coat. Baker wanted to tell him to go to hell, but he was too tired to work up the anger needed.

A line appeared between Seth's eyebrows. "Are you not talking to me because you can't or because you don't want to? I'm your doctor. I need to know."

"I'd like a new doctor."

A smile exploded across Seth's face. "Too bad. You're my friend, so you're stuck with me."

Baker closed his eyes. He wanted to go back to sleep. "I'd hate to see how you treat your enemies."

. . .

"I don't have any enemies."

Baker bit his tongue before admitting Seth had one now.

"Seriously. How are you feeling?"

In an attempt to beat back his irritation, Baker swallowed a sigh. "Like I got hit by a truck."

"I don't doubt it. Do you know what happened to you?"

He could do this. Baker could force Seth to stay in his professional role. Seth was his doctor. Baker was the patient. That was all. Plus, he really needed to know why he felt so horrid. "I had a heart attack."

Seth rubbed his stethoscope, warming it before listening to Baker's heart. "Actually, you suffered a second heart event an hour after you were admitted. Your cardiologist had to put in a stent. They went in through the groin, so that'll hurt like a bitch when the meds wear off."

Baker took another look around. He was in a different room. That fucked with his head more than he wanted to admit. The last time he had fallen asleep, he had been watching his vitals inside a trauma room. This looked like a regular hospital room. There were flowers nearby and a huge cup of water. Panic set in.

"How long have I been here?"

"Aric brought you in yesterday around lunch time. It's six p.m. now. You've been in and out. I sent Aric home about an hour ago. He had a few things to say to me about it, but he went."

Baker took a few steadying breaths. He needed to wake up. He had responsibilities. There was a law firm with his name on the door that needed his attention. "I need to call Joshua and get someone working on my caseload."

Seth's eyebrows rose. "You'll do no such thing. Aric has taken care of everything. Right now, your life is all about resting. Just let me take care of you. It's fine to be selfish and focus on recovery. This is serious business, Baker. You almost died."

Baker grabbed Seth's words and used them against him. "If I'm being selfish and resting, then you should go. I'll have Aric find me another doctor."

"Stop." Seth looked serious and sad, drawing Baker's raging thoughts up short. "I know you're mad at me. Aric made it abundantly clear that I'm the asshole. You can say all that to me later. Right now, just take a breath. It's time to rest."

. . .

Admittedly, Baker was tired. He didn't feel up to fighting. His head told him he was enraged, but his body was too weak. He took a breath.

"Get some sleep. I'll be here when you wake up." As if to punctuate his claim, Seth sat in a nearby chair.

Baker didn't have it in him to argue. He closed his eyes, but all he felt was Seth's stare. "It's really hard to sleep with you sitting here, looking at me."

"Do I need to order you something to help you sleep?"

A snort escaped Baker without thought. "Cheeky bastard."

A sexy chuckle rumbled from Seth. Baker kept his eyes squeezed shut, hoping Seth wouldn't see how much he hurt. He knew they weren't together, and Seth didn't owe him anything. The thing was, Baker thought he meant a little more than Seth being with someone else literally hours after leaving his bed. Maybe Baker was a romantic, but fuck.

"What are you thinking about? Your heartbeat and blood pressure are rising too much."

Baker swallowed past the pain. "It doesn't matter."

"It does to me."

Baker's eyelids felt so heavy. He couldn't make it stop. "I don't matter to anyone." The words sounded groggy even to Baker's ears. He had never been more exhausted. His brain refused to cling to a single thought. There was no chance of him staying awake. If Seth wanted to watch him sleep, so be it. Baker had nothing left to give.

Years ago, Seth had decided to live his life as unapologetically as possible. Chrissy had been the only person in the family who hadn't traumatized him with religion, swearing to love the sinner and hate the sin while continually telling him he would burn in hell. Even though his parents had been gone for years, Seth held tight to his bitterness and refused to do anything that might have pleased his parents. Even being a doctor, Seth had weaponized against them. His dad had been a respected family practitioner. He expected the same respectability of Seth. So Seth went a different direction, becoming a doctor to the stars, determined to be the black sheep until the day he died.

For the first time in his life, Seth felt a hint of guilt. In his pursuit to be the constant disappointment, he realized how he had hurt Baker. Worse than that, he had made Baker feel unimportant. He didn't know why he was like this. Seth's anger just ran so damn deep. No matter what he had done or said, his parents had refused to see how beating their son to death with the Bible had damaged him. They had taught him to hate the idea of love, because theirs had been so toxic. Now all he did was hurt people.

. . .

I don't matter to anyone.

Those words rang so deeply, they resonated in Seth's soul. Baker thought Seth didn't care at all, and that was Seth's fault. It also wasn't true. Seth headed out into the hall and pulled his phone from the pocket of his doctor's coat. He started by calling in a few favors to get his patients covered by various doctors around town for the next few weeks. Then he hired a friend to get started on finding Kye some help. He didn't want to replace Kye, but he also couldn't pretend Kye wasn't leaving while they had such a huge patient load. For now, he genuinely didn't know how to fix that part of his life. Kye quitting had sideswiped him. Seth needed more than two weeks to figure out that mess.

With his plate emptied for the next few weeks, Seth went to work on Baker's chart, making a plan for them to work closely together over the next couple of weeks to get Baker back to good health. Seth didn't think Baker's diet, or a lack of exercise, was to blame.

He thought Baker took on too much stress. That included Seth, but Seth's brain shied away from that truth.

When it couldn't be avoided any longer, Seth searched Baker's file and found Aric's number. He needed to mend that fence if he ever hoped to get back on Baker's good side.

Aric answered on the first ring, as if waiting for a call. "Hello?"

"Aric? This is Dr. Black."

"Is Baker all right?"

At the panic in Aric's voice, Seth raced to reassure him. "Yes. He's resting. I'm calling because I've decided to take a couple of weeks away from my practice to ensure Baker is properly on the mend and I could use your help."

. . .

His words were met with heavy skepticism. "Go on."

This was where he needed to skate a thin line. "Baker will be coming home with me until he's able to take care of himself without overdoing things, which we both know won't happen without a constant guard. My fear is, without you, he will still try to do more than he should. How do you feel about working from my place the next couple of weeks for triple your usual pay?"

For a moment, Aric said nothing. When he finally responded, he sounded resigned. "Baker has no clue he'll be going home with you, does he?"

Seth couldn't lie. "Not yet."

"He won't go." The surety in Aric's voice couldn't be missed.

. . .

Seth had no intention of backing down. "He will if you will."

"Hard pass." Aric's immediate decision had Seth putting it all on the line.

"Look, I know you have no reason to believe me, but I care about Baker as much as you do. I just lost my sister, and I don't have many people left. Baker is coming home with me and he's getting better whether he likes it or not. If he wants to hate me for it afterward, so be it. At least I'll know he's alive somewhere in the world. He can even keep the pieces of my heart he's stolen when he goes. Will you help me or not?"

Aric blew out a breath. "When do you need me there?"

Seth fought the urge to smile. He didn't want Aric to hear it in his voice. "Likely it'll be a few days. If that changes, I'll let you know."

. . .

"Okay. I'll be there."

"Thank you." Even Seth heard the relief in his voice.

Aric didn't let him get too comfortable. "I'm only agreeing to this because I love Baker and I want him better. But if I think for one second that you're making him worse, he's coming home with me. Understood?"

Seth nodded, even though Aric couldn't see him. "Understood."

"I'll see you at the hospital in the morning then." Aric disconnected their call before Seth could respond.

Seth slipped his phone back in his pocket and headed back to Baker's bedside. He already knew he had a long battle ahead of him. Baker would likely put up a way bigger fight than Aric. Seth was ready. Whatever it took, he would make Baker well and then he would prove he wasn't a piece of shit. Maybe Seth didn't understand why he felt so much for Baker, but he would figure it out. There had to be a reason it hurt his chest to think of Baker seeing him with someone else. Seth had to know. Baker was too important. Seth couldn't walk away.

SEVEN

"WOULD YOU LIKE A DRINK?"

Baker couldn't stop following Seth with his gaze, waiting for the perfect moment to pounce. "No."

Seth's mouth lifted in one corner in a sexy smirk. "You look hungry."

"I am. Where's your bedroom?"

. . .

Baker blinked at his unfamiliar surroundings. The last wisps of his dream slipped away. For a moment, he stared at the walls of Seth's bedroom, wondering if it hadn't been a dream after all. Then the past week came back to him. That still didn't explain how he'd ended up in Seth's bed. He rolled and found Seth sleeping next to him. His confusion doubled. The last thing he remembered was being in the hospital. He tried to sit up, but Seth's arm shot out, curled around him, and hauled him closer. Then his leg draped over Baker's hip, pinning him to the bed.

"Good morning, gorgeous."

Seth sounded groggy and hot as hell. Baker's body immediately responded, as if he didn't feel half dead. He had to clear his throat to speak. "Um. How am I in your bed?"

One blue eye opened to stare at him. "I had you transported here."

.   .   .

No shame. Not a single ounce of remorse tinged Seth's confession. "You did what?"

"I almost lost you. That's not happening on my watch. You'll stay here until I know you're healed."

Baker glanced behind him. "Where's my phone? I need to call Aric to come get me."

Seth snuggled closer. "Aric is right out front, helping Kye. If you need him, all you have to do is yell."

The sense of betrayal that washed over Baker was epic. "What? Aric would never team up with you against me."

At his claim, Seth looked fully awake. "Damn. You must really hate me if you think Aric wanting you alive is a betrayal. All because he knows I can make you better."

· · ·

The guilt hit hard. He didn't understand how Seth could tie him up in knots like this all the time. Baker was self-aware. He knew Seth would destroy him. Yet he willingly walked into the fire every damn time.

He chose to attack from a different angle. "You could've asked instead of drugging me and kidnapping me."

Seth's puzzled expression had Baker's stomach twisting into knots. "I didn't do either of those things. You haven't been able to stay awake for longer than five minutes all week. I fully intended to tell you everything, but you slept through the transfer. Aric was there the entire time, ensuring you were treated properly."

Fuck. Baker's head was such a mess. He needed to get his body onboard with his mind because he was out of there. "I need a shower."

. . .

Seth nodded. "That's fine. I can supervise."

It was hard, but Baker suppressed his eye roll. "No, thank you. I'd rather have Aric."

Seth snorted. "If you pass out, there's no way Aric could catch you. He's so tiny. You'd crush him. Suck it up. I've seen you naked."

With his teeth gritted, Baker gave Seth a sharp nod. If he hoped to win the war, sacrifices must be made. Once Baker had his shower, he would feel human again. Once he felt human again, he was out of there.

With his agreement in place, Seth rolled from the bed and gently helped Baker to his feet. Until Baker was upright, he didn't realize how weak he felt. He held tighter to Seth for support. By the time they made it to the bathroom, he was out of breath. Seth helped him through all sorts of embarrassment before leading him into the shower. Baker hadn't realized how much his bodily functions would make themselves known the moment he was on his feet.

Inside the shower, he sat on the bench while Seth warmed the water. The moment hot water hit his skin; Baker sighed in relief. He closed his eyes and let Seth take care of him. It was humiliating, but Baker never intended to see Seth again once this was over. He would get Aric to take him home and then hand his work off to someone else. That included the handling of Chrissy's estate. He already had a cardiologist. All he needed to do was find another primary care doctor. Then he could close the door on his relationship with Seth. Surely he could have that handled by the end of the day.

Exhaustion weighed heavily on Baker's shoulders while Seth scrubbed his hair. His head bobbed, making him realize he dozed. Baker blinked against the weariness. Baker dropped his gaze, and the state of his body caught his attention. In a distant sort of way, he had known he had a heart attack, and they had done surgery, further wearing him down. He hadn't realized until now how messed up he looked.

It was depressing. Nothing made him recognize he needed to give up the dream of Seth like seeing the weight he had lost and the odd coloration to his skin. If only he could stay awake, Baker would demand to go home. The problem was, he was too tired to fight.

Seth's mind was a mess. Baker kept dozing off, and Seth tried his damnedest to get him clean as fast as possible. The problem was, he couldn't stop touching Baker. By the time he had Baker back in bed, Baker was completely out, and Seth worried Baker would never look at him again with anything other than hatred. That wasn't an outcome Seth could live with.

After checking Baker's vitals, Seth ran through his morning routine. He went through the motions of working out before taking a shower. Seth assured himself one more time Baker slept peacefully before heading to the kitchen. He had always enjoyed cooking. When he had his house built, he had made sure the kitchen was huge with plenty of cabinets and countertop space. Seth like to spread out and make too much food. This morning, he kept things simple since he needed to get back to Baker as quickly as possible. Juice, fruit, whole wheat toast, and eggs should be enough. Baker still wasn't eating much. Seth needed to fix that.

He carried the tray to the bedroom, moving as quickly as possible. Each time he left Baker alone, Seth experienced a hint of panic. He was scared as hell he would come back and find Baker had left... or had passed. Seth damn near had to stop halfway to the bedroom so he could set the tray aside and brace his hands on his knees to properly hyperventilate. Seth didn't have time for that now.

On the way to his room, he passed Kye. Kye quickly changed directions and headed back into the sanctuary of his office. Seth blew out a sigh. He didn't know how to fix things. Kye hadn't talked to him like a friend in years. He knew he needed to figure out how to get Kye to stay, but he didn't know where to start. Seth was spread too thin all the time. It was possible he just needed to let Kye go. Seth had done the best he could to make Kye's final two weeks with him as easy as possible. He had hired two new

NPs to take over Kye's patients. Well, a friend of his had done the hiring, but Kye was free of that. Kye had Aric helping him around the office, setting everything up for a new hire. Seth had a temporary service sending someone to take over Kye's office duties. At his bedroom door, Seth stopped and took a breath. Maybe he needed to retire. Seth's eyes fell closed. He hated that thought, but Seth didn't know what else to do. His practice had gotten too big for Kye and him to handle. He should pass his patients along. Damn. He genuinely didn't know when his life had gotten so fucked up.

With his heart heavy, Seth slipped back inside the bedroom. To his surprise, Baker was sitting up with a pillow pressed to his chest, trying to cough. Seth rushed to his side. After setting the tray aside, he sat on the edge of the bed. He readjusted the pillow and did his best to help. As much as it pained him, Seth knew he had to let Baker do this part on his own. Baker couldn't let his lungs fill with fluid.

Baker took a few audible breaths. "Sorry. I don't know what happened."

. . .

Seth grabbed his stethoscope and listened to Baker's lungs. They sounded clear. "Don't apologize. Your body is doing exactly what it should be to keep fluid from building up in your lungs. If you can stay sitting up for a little while, that'll help a lot. Are you ready for breakfast?"

Baker nodded and Seth moved the tray to the bed. While eyeing the food, Baker kept up his end of the conversation. "Thank you for this. I really don't understand why this happened to me. I play tennis regularly and try to stick to a decent diet. Plus, I'm only a month from forty-one. It makes no sense."

Seth nodded along and tried to answer the best he could. "Stress will kill you faster than the worst of lifestyles. When was the last time you took any time off or relaxed at all?"

Baker took a bite of toast before responding. "I could ask the same of you."

. . .

That was true, except for one key difference. "I don't think I take life as seriously as you do. Not that it's a bad thing," Seth rushed to add. "Your job requires a constant businesslike demeanor, but you hold on to it even when you're not working. I'd love to see you take a breath."

For a moment, Baker ate in silence while staring at nothing, as if lost in his head. Finally, he focused on Seth. "I suppose I am the way you describe. My brother and I were very much seen and not heard growing up. The only way we were allowed to express an opinion was if we could hold an intellectual conversation on the matter."

"I didn't know you had a brother."

Baker nodded. "Phillip. He's two years my junior. I haven't seen him in quite some time. He has a practice in Brighton and doesn't come this way often."

. . .

Seth hated that. Having just lost his sister, he was extra sensitive to family separation. "Does he know you've been in the hospital?"

Baker sipped his juice. "It's not as if he could drop everything and skip across the pond. There's no sense in worrying him."

Seth shook his head. He truly didn't understand Baker. It was as if Baker didn't want anyone to care about him—like he feared inconveniencing anyone. Seth needed Baker to know he had Seth. "Well, I'm here and plan to take good care of you."

Baker chuckled. "I look forward to your hefty bill. What's the charge for being in your bed?"

Something inside Seth snapped closed. "You must really think terribly of me."

. . .

Baker set his drink aside. He didn't meet Seth's gaze directly. "Not at all. I think you're a brilliant doctor."

"I meant personally."

A sad smile touched Baker's lips. "No. I get it. You had a choice between this," Baker waved absently toward himself, "and someone half my age. What shot did I have, really? No one would've chosen me in that race. I'm tired. I think I'd like to go back to sleep now."

It hit Seth. Not all of Baker's exhaustion was related to his heart. Baker was also deeply unhappy. Seth dropped his gaze to the tray to hide the way his discovery punched him in the throat. Baker had only eaten half the toast and drank a quarter of the juice. Everything else was untouched.

"Drink your juice first. I can't have you getting dehydrated." Seth waited until Baker lifted the glass to his lips to continue. "I had lunch plans with

Larkin for two weeks before I spent the day in your bed."

"Larkin? Fuck. Even his name is twenty years younger than me."

Seth ignored Baker's interruption. "By the time I left your bed, it was too late to cancel without being a total ass. I didn't see the harm, since it was only lunch. I figured I'd go, enjoy a meal, and then part on good terms. Sex wasn't even on the table. You had already completely drained me. I had hoped that I would see you again that night and take you to dinner. You deserve a real date."

"Two dates in one day. How fantastic for you."

Seth continued ignoring Baker's jibes. "Obviously, I didn't get to take you out, but I haven't given up hope. I like you, Baker. A lot. I'd like to be more than friends." Seth knew his timing was terrible, but he couldn't have Baker fighting him every step of his healing.

Baker froze with his glass halfway to his mouth.

Seth forged on. "You don't have to answer me right now. I just need you to know that I would choose you over anyone else. I am choosing you."

"I don't know what to say."

The realization of exactly how horrible his timing was washed over Seth. He made a dismissive motion. "Don't say anything. Drink your juice. Then go back to sleep. After you've had a nap, we'll practice walking around the room."

Baker polished off his juice. "We can try now, if you want. I'm oddly wide awake now."

. . .

That made Seth happier than he planned to show. He didn't want Baker to change his mind. "I know you're not usually seen in public wearing your pj pants and a t-shirt, but how do you feel about strolling down the hall to Kye's office to see Aric?"

Baker visibly brightened. "I'd like that."

Seth quickly moved the tray so he could help Baker to his feet. Once he was up, Baker did better this time than he had on the way to the shower. He let Baker lean into his side and hold his arm as he led Baker to Kye's office. Kye and the usual delivery guy —who Seth had learned was named Sonny—were near the front door, flirting. Well, Kye was flirting. Sonny was blushing.

"Adorable," Baker said beneath his breath, making Seth smile.

.   .   .

"Yeah. I think Kye is still wearing him down. The poor guy is still in disbelief that Kye actually likes him."

"He's a good person. At least, that's what Aric tells me, and Aric is a very good judge of character."

Baker sounded tired, but he kept moving. Seth slowed his pace just to be safe. The moment Aric spotted Baker on his feet, he lit from the inside. Seth felt Baker stiffen his spine, as if he couldn't look weak and worry Aric.

"Oh my god. You're upright." Aric shot to his feet and bounded their way. He stopped short of running Baker over. Instead, he kissed Baker's cheek before finding him a chair.

Seth stood watch while the pair chatted. Aric updated Baker on work, making sure he relaxed and understood everything was under control. Throughout their conversation, they told each other several times they loved each other. Seth caught himself rubbing his chest. He didn't have what they did with anyone. It was depressing as hell.

Exhaustion hit from nowhere, making Baker's eyelids heavy. He almost fell asleep mid conversation. Seth helped him to his feet again.

"Come on, gorgeous. No overdoing it on my watch."

Baker blinked as he looked Seth's way. He looked sad. From nowhere, Baker experienced a moment of deep connection with Seth. Seth wanted to be more than friends. He had always been honest with Baker, even if he didn't think Baker would like what he had to say. Baker didn't know how to feel. He hadn't forgotten the deep hurt and jealousy he had felt at seeing Seth with someone else. Baker was torn in two.

. . .

Aric reassured him he would be around, and Seth led Baker back to bed. After taking his meds, he was half asleep before his head hit the pillow.

Then Seth's lips brushed his. Until that moment, Baker had been in more pain than he cared to admit. It was like Seth's kiss had healing powers. A steadying breath filled his lungs. Baker swore his blood pressure lowered. He knew he should set some boundaries with Seth, but he wasn't sure he wanted to. His worn-out body didn't care about his mixed feelings or any drama happening in his life. He fell asleep.

EIGHT

EVERY DAY, Baker got stronger. Seth went a little crazier. They slept beside each other each night. Each morning, Seth woke wrapped in Baker's embrace. They never talked about it. Occasionally, Baker would tolerate Seth brushing his lips across Baker's. Baker was strong enough to shower alone, but he still let Seth bathe him. In fact, Baker was strong enough to go home, but they never talked about that either. Seth knew their time together was quickly drawing to a close. The hard part was accepting it.

Baker had started hanging out in Kye's office a few hours a day, doing some light work from there with

Aric. Those hours gave Seth time to see a few patients and settle some things. He had told no one other than the affected patients, but he spent those few hours each day letting his patients know personally he would soon partially retire. They would need to hunt for a new physician. No one liked to hear that. Seth couldn't end up making himself sick the way Baker had. He couldn't deny he had been working himself into the grave every bit as much as Baker had been. Seth had a handful of friends he would continue to see as patients. There were a few others he would still make emergency calls for, but otherwise, he needed to slow down. It was time to admit he had been overworking to keep from being alone with his feelings. Seth wouldn't avoid emotional ties any longer.

Kye's two-week notice had passed without note, and he hadn't left. Seth knew he was biding his time until Baker was healed. He didn't pretend Kye would stay. That was okay. Seth had made peace with Kye's resignation. He understood he had neglected Kye too long and didn't deserve him. That didn't mean Seth didn't have a plan to set things as right as he could.

Even if Kye left, Seth needed to know Kye wasn't out there somewhere, hating him.

Seth made his way to Kye's office. His heart drew him there. As he rounded the corner, he spotted Baker seated next to Aric. Their heads were together, looking at something on Aric's phone. Their closeness never ceased to fill Seth with wonderment and a hint of jealousy. He didn't have that type of relationship with anyone any longer. Not since Chrissy passed. He doubted anyone else would ever see past his bullshit the way she had. That thought made his chest hurt. He quickly moved to insert himself in Baker and Aric's world to save himself from the drowning sensation.

Seth bent and kissed the side of Baker's neck. "Hey there, sexy. What are two of my favorite people working on today?"

Aric leaned away and hid his phone.

. . .

Baker flashed him a smile. "We were shopping online for a gift for Aric's husband."

Seth nodded along. "Your husband is the tall guy who owns The Aviator, right?"

Aric's gaze met Seth's. He looked surprised Seth had remembered that. "Yes. I want to buy him something special. Unfortunately, he's super hard to buy for because he never talks about wanting anything."

The night Seth had taken Baker home for the first time, he had seen Aric and his husband together. The guy looked at Aric like he would starve without him. Another hint of jealousy wormed its way in. No one would ever look at him like that either. He had pretty much turned his life into a shit show a long time ago just to piss off his father. Now, he didn't know how to make it stop. Seth refused to get swallowed whole today by the bitterness.

. . .

"I've seen how that man looks at you. You should wrap yourself in nothing but a ribbon and let him unwrap you. I promise you he would declare it the best gift ever." Aric blushed, but Seth didn't wait to hear his thoughts. He turned his attention Baker's way. "It's time for your daily exercise."

Baker groaned. "I'm not loving this daily nonsense. You know I'm a tennis player. This other boorish business is not for me."

Seth's smile was out of his control. He loved being in Baker's company. "If you want to get back to those tennis games, you have to put in the work."

"But I loathe the treadmill. It's so monotonous."

Seth pulled Baker to his feet. "Don't worry. I have a different plan for you today."

. . .

Baker's expression immediately turned suspicious. His eyebrows drew together. "What type of plan?"

With a chuckle, Seth led Baker down the hall. "It's a surprise."

Baker didn't look any less doubtful. "As someone whose heart recently stopped, I have to say I'm not fond of surprises."

He couldn't promise Baker would like this one, but he hoped Baker would. After leading Baker down the hall, Seth opened the door to his ballroom. It was one of the many rooms in the house that never got used. When Seth had built the place twenty years ago, his mom had insisted he would need room to entertain. It turned out to be wasted space. Today, he found its purpose.

Slow rock poured from unseen speakers. Just as Seth had set them up to do. Baker glanced his way as they crossed the threshold. He still looked confused.

. . .

Seth swept Baker into his arms and pulled him close. "I can't let you leave here until I know you're well enough to get back to everyday life."

The way Baker smiled had the knots in Seth's shoulders relaxing. "And you think slow dancing with men is everyday life for me?"

"It should be," Seth answered honestly. "At least, you should do this more often with me, anyhow."

To Seth's surprise, Baker shuffled closer. Seth had expected at least a small argument. Instead, Baker buried his face against the crook of Seth's neck and let Seth lead. Seth's heart squeezed as Baker's lips lightly brushed his skin. He had given Baker every reason to hate him. Yet Baker still openly showed Seth affection. Seth didn't deserve it. Baker was this beautiful open-to-anything bisexual. Seth was the self-hating gay. He was the guy who threw his sexuality in everyone's faces, hoping to weed out the people who were like his father. At least, that was how it started. Somewhere along the way, he had turned into a seducer. One with zero respect for anything or anyone, especially himself. Then Baker had quietly accepted him as the piece of shit he was, and cared about him anyway. Now Seth wanted to deserve his faith.

Seth held Baker a little tighter. "I have a confession. You've been strong enough to go home for days."

He felt Baker's lips shape into a smile against his skin. "I suppose I should also confess I knew that. If I'd wanted to go home, you wouldn't have been able to stop me."

Seth's heart beat a little faster. His palms began to sweat. He recognized how serious their conversation became. Seth could stop now and go back to being the guy who cared about no one. He didn't want that.

. . .

In his nervousness, Seth licked his lips. "What if..." Seth took a breath and started again. "What if you just stayed?"

"What if I did?" Baker asked, making Seth want to scream in his moment of desperation.

"That's what I'm saying. What if you stayed?"

He felt Baker smile against his skin again. "Do you want me to stay?"

Seth took another breath. It sounded ragged, even with the music muffling it. He had never been more terrified. "Yes. I think I would like that very much."

"Then I suppose I'm staying."

Seth didn't think. He simply turned his head and captured Baker's lips. Seth didn't know what he felt, but he knew it was powerful and he couldn't let Baker get away. He also didn't know how long Baker would let him keep him. Seth would take as much as he could get.

———

There was a very good chance Baker was an idiot. Even he couldn't explain why he kept falling for Seth. The thing was, he had been under Seth's roof for a couple of weeks and in his bed every night. Seth didn't text other men or sleep anywhere else. Every night, Baker found himself wrapping his arms around Seth, pretending a little more this was real. Somewhere along the line, he accidentally convinced himself it was true. Baker might be stupid, but he wasn't ignorant. He knew Seth would likely make him sorry. Baker just wasn't so sure he cared any longer. If he didn't take this chance, Baker would regret Seth for the rest of his life. If Baker had one talent, it was giving people a million chances to destroy him. That probably would never change, so there was no reason to deny himself this.

"Do you mind if we go back to bed now?"

. . .

Seth immediately stopped dancing and eyed Baker with concern. "Are you okay? Did you overdo it this morning while I was gone?"

Baker shook his head. "That's not why I want to go to bed with you."

He watched realization dawn in Seth's expression. "I don't know if you're ready for quite that much activity."

A smile that felt wicked even to him stretched Baker's lips. "I guess you'll have to do all the work, then."

While holding his stare, Seth drew Baker closer and whisked his lips across Baker's. Baker held his breath, waiting. Seth lightly kissed him again, sweetly brushing his lips back and forth across Baker's. A feeling washed over Baker he didn't expect. In a moment of complete clarity, Baker realized why he kept letting Seth have chances he didn't deserve. Being with Seth felt a lot like love, and Baker wanted it to be true. It was scary how much of himself he was willing to give, just to be loved back.

Seth's hands found Baker's ass. "I want your word you'll do nothing and let me be in control."

Baker's body already burned. There was nothing he wouldn't have promised in that moment. "You have it."

"If you feel any pressure in your chest, you have to swear you'll tell me so I can stop."

A laugh burst from Baker. He couldn't help it. Seth was adorable. "It's almost as if you don't trust me."

He felt Seth's muscles relax. "I can't lose you."

· · ·

The laughter died in Baker's throat at Seth's serious tone. He had a fire in his eyes Baker hadn't expected. It hit Baker. Seth cared. He genuinely felt something for Baker, whether or not he recognized it. The realization had Baker wanting more.

He unbuttoned Seth's jeans. "I swear to you I'm not going anywhere. Nothing is coming between me and my shot at finally keeping you to myself for as long as you'll have me. I want you, but I want time with you more."

Without a word, Seth grabbed Baker's hand and stormed from the room. He was a man on a mission. Baker was here for it. He fought a laugh as Seth dragged him into the bedroom and kicked the door closed behind them.

His laughter turned breathless as Seth tore at his clothes. Their mouths clashed, only parting long enough to lose more clothing. When their nude bodies touched, Baker sucked in a breath. God. He knew his heart, and Baker was in love with this man.

All those weeks he had craved any word from Seth came back to haunt him. Desperation crawled up Baker's throat, forcing him to swallow words Seth wasn't ready to hear. They had known each other a long time. Their friendship had become something new Baker didn't want to live without. He needed Seth.

Seth's fury seemed to slow. He eased Baker down onto the bed. Baker stayed still and tried not to over-excite his heart while Seth kissed a path down his body. The incision they had made at his groin during surgery was still tender. Seth made him comfortable even as he licked Baker's cock. While Baker floated on a cloud of lust, Seth moved away and quickly returned with lube and condoms. Baker did what Seth made him promise he would do. He relaxed and enjoyed handing over control.

Baker let Seth put a condom on him and lube the outside. When Seth returned to claim his mouth, Baker was ready. He wanted all of Seth's kisses and more. Seth lingered over Baker's mouth, stealing more pieces of Baker's heart. Baker knew this time it was about more than sex. They were both there because they didn't want to be with anyone else. That was a powerful feeling. It was the kind of feeling that could leave Baker addicted.

Then Seth sat on Baker's dick. Baker saw stars. He wanted to move, but he had promised he wouldn't. Baker stayed still while Seth lifted and dropped, gently riding Baker's cock. He held Baker's stare while taking his pleasure. In that moment, Baker knew Seth was the one. He had never been more connected with anyone. If Seth decided this wasn't what he wanted, it would crush Baker. But Baker still wouldn't regret him. Some things were worth the risk.

Pressure slowly climbed Baker's shaft, making him insane. He had to force himself to stay still. Seth's expression ending up saving him. His lips were parted and swollen. Seth's cheeks were flushed. He looked exactly like a man on the edge of orgasm. Baker wanted to watch it happen. Seth tried kissing him. Baker held him away so he could watch him come. Only once Seth's cum hit Baker's chest did

Baker pull him down and claim his mouth while Seth's greedy asshole pulled an orgasm from Baker.

Baker scratched at Seth's skin as the pleasure rocked him. In that moment, Baker saw everything with perfect clarity. They weren't some epic love story with raging highs and lows. They were adults who didn't always see themselves as clearly as they liked, but they were getting there. Baker was smart enough to know a good thing. He believed all the way to his soul that Seth was the same. A lot of people might not understand them, but they got each other. Sometimes love was a quiet acceptance of the inevitable. Baker was okay with that.

After Seth cleaned them and they were settled into each other's arms, Baker realized how much he loved this part of them. They always cuddled. Not even when he thought they were only a one-night stand did either of them rush away. They had held each other all night that night too. Baker wondered if that was the part he hadn't been able to get past after that night. Sex could be found anywhere. This connection couldn't.

.   .   .

"I don't know what to do about Kye."

Baker didn't need Seth to expound. Seth was losing his friend. Baker also wasn't upset Seth's thoughts were on another man while holding him. He felt special—like he was Seth's safe space.

All Baker could do was offer him the best advice he could. "He just wants his hard work and loyalty acknowledged. I imagine he also would like to stop working himself into an early grave. If you can find a way to get past that, you're golden. No one has as much anger as Kye does unless it first comes from a place of love."

"He doesn't have to worry about working himself into the ground any longer. I'm going into partial retirement."

.   .   .

Seth's confession rocked Baker. He hadn't seen that one coming. "Okay. Wow. What made you decide that?"

He felt Seth shrug. "I guess I realized some things about myself I don't like. Between Kye quitting and hurting you, I had to stop and take a moment. I didn't like what I saw. I don't want Kye to work himself into an early grave, and I don't want to pretend I don't want a normal life any longer."

Baker didn't want to bring up the past, but he had to be honest. "Is that what you were doing? Because you looked pretty happy with your life and that guy half your age."

Seth's gaze met Baker's.

The hurt in his eyes had Baker explaining. "I'm not throwing that day in your face. I'm genuinely curious. Were you unhappy with your life?"

· · ·

Seth didn't look away. "The only time I'm happy is when I'm with you."

Baker's heart melted. He was such an easy mark.

Seth didn't stop there. "I don't want to go back to working nonstop and pretending to be someone I'm not. The thought of that makes me feel sick. I want Kye to be young and happy. I want you."

Even as he basked in Seth's confession, he mulled over Seth's problem. Kye had a lot of anger in him. Baker had won him over with flowers, but Kye didn't have any real contempt for Baker. His issues with Seth ran deep. "You'll have to go big. I think you'll have to go all or nothing if you hope to truly win back your friendship with Kye. He's had a lot of years to fester."

Seth nodded. "I have an idea, but I'll need your help."

. . .

"Anything." Baker meant it from the bottom of his soul. They were building something together, but first, it stood on friendship. They were partners. Baker had never had this before. He immediately knew it was right. Being with Seth put all his previous relationships to shame. This was the best kind of love.

NINE

AFTER AN AMAZING NIGHT with Baker turned into a perfect morning, Seth finally forced himself from the bed. Baker had made some calls and put a rush on Seth's plans to save his friendship with Kye. With the paperwork delivered, Seth went over the fine print, under the guise of reading Kye's patient reports, while Kye flirted with the delivery guy.

In a chair outside Kye's office, Seth flipped through each page, seeing nothing. He knew this was the right decision. That wasn't why an overwhelming wave of sadness tried pulling him under. It was grief. Despite preparing himself for years to lose his sister, the loss was still fresh. He had been too busy with

Baker to fully process. Occasionally, grief jumped out from the recesses of his mind and sucker punched him in the throat. He tried catching his breath.

It wasn't fair that her life had been cut short. He wished she was here to see him fall for Baker. Seth wanted to confide his excitement. He missed their talks. Every day, Seth had called her about this time. They would talk for close to an hour about nothing. Each day, he still pulled out his phone before reality slapped him again. He had moments of panic in his absent mindedness, where he thought he had forgotten to call, only to be reminded again. Grief was an endless cycle. Baker was his only saving grace.

Seth's gaze moved Kye's way. Talking to Baker about Kye last night made Seth understand what it was about Baker. They were friends first. That was their foundation. They could talk about anything and come out stronger and better for it. That was how he knew this was the right decision. Seth went back to reading. Soon, he would know if he had lost Kye for good or not with his selfishness. Seth wasn't sure he was ready.

Kye had been shipping ridiculous things he could simply drive across town for months now, trying to get Sonny to notice him. He had never had this big of a crush before. The guy had arms the size of Kye's thighs and a thick beard that gave Kye all the naughty thoughts. Sonny was genuinely sweet, and Kye had never wanted to ride someone's face so badly in his entire life.

Today was the first day Kye thought he might have a chance. He rolled the stem of the flower Sonny had picked for him between his fingers and tried not to smile like an idiot. "This is beautiful. Thank you."

Sonny blushed. His brown eyes shone bright with kindness. "I saw it on my lunch break, and it made me think of you."

.   .   .

Damn. He reminded everyone of flowers lately. Kye didn't get it. There was nothing delicate about him, but he liked people thought of him that way. Kye had been waiting forever for Sonny to ask him out, but he never did. The guy was so shy, Kye worried he would say no if Kye asked first. Plus, Kye hadn't been on a date in ages. If Sonny said no, Kye didn't know if his self-esteem would recover. But the guy wasn't budging. Kye had to do something.

"There's a package in my office. Do you mind helping me?"

Sonny straightened away from the counter he had been leaning on to his full six-six glory. "Sure. Lead the way."

Kye took a steadying breath and headed for his office. He could feel Sonny at his back. His nerves frayed. Today's package was tiny as hell, but it was the best Kye could come up with to keep Sonny a few moments longer today and to get him alone.

· · ·

Kye spoke over his shoulder as he went. "I don't know if I've told you, but I'm on my last few days here."

"No, he isn't," Seth yelled from his nearby seat where he went over Kye's patient notes.

Kye rolled his eyes. "Yes, I am. He just hasn't accepted reality yet."

Sonny looked defeated. "Really? This is my favorite stop."

It was now or never. "About that." Kye closed his office door behind Sonny so they could have some privacy. He set his flower on the desk and grabbed the minuscule package. Kye passed it Sonny's way. "I've been thinking. How do you feel about—"

Sonny kissed him. There was no warning or lead-up. One second Kye was shooting his shot, the next Kye was lifted onto his desk and clinging to Sonny's massive shoulders while he got completely invaded. It was... holy shit. Kye had never felt tinier. Sonny's teeth sank into Kye's bottom lip and nibbled. Kye heard himself pant. It was out of his control. He had never been more instantly ready to get fucked in all his life. He might have begged. Kye couldn't be sure. His entire mind was blown by the heat between them.

The office door opened. "Hey, Kye. I need to talk..."

Sonny leaped away from Kye. He held the tiny package in front of his crotch and inched toward the door.

Seth's gaze moved between Kye and Sonny. He focused on the small box Sonny held. "Yeah. That's not hiding anything."

. . .

Just when Kye thought Sonny couldn't get redder, Seth's pointing out of the obvious had Sonny twice as red as an apple.

Kye refused to be embarrassed. "So I'll see you here tonight when you get off for dinner?"

Sonny's gaze moved Kye's way. All embarrassment fled Sonny's expression when he looked Kye's way. "It'll probably be close to seven."

Kye nodded. "That's fine. I'll see you then."

With a sharp nod, Sonny eased out the door. Kye watched him go with all the hunger in his heart. Surely he could make it until seven. After all, he had waited months to get this far. Kye fought a whimper. Seven couldn't get here soon enough. Kye needed more.

Seth sort of wanted to make himself invisible. The heat Kye flashed toward the retreating delivery man was off the charts. The thing was, Kye's remark about leaving meant he couldn't wait any longer to try to make things right. He had thought long and hard about how to fix things. Only one thing felt right. Seth's mind was set.

"Sorry to interrupt."

Kye tore his gaze away from Sonny's retreating form and focused on Seth. "No worries. I understand this isn't the place." He pressed his hands against his overheated cheeks. "I don't know what happened."

"Lust and close proximity. It happens. Anyhow," Seth said, determined to move past any office indiscretions. "I've had some time to think, and I've made some huge decisions that will affect us both."

Kye held up his hand, stopping Seth. "I don't need to hear anything else. Friday is my last day. Any

146

decisions you've made will have to wait for the next guy. None of it affects me."

"Actually, that's not true." Seth held a stack of papers out to Kye.

Kye took them. "Have you finished going through the patient notes, alr—" Kye glanced down at the papers. His eyebrows snapped together as he read. Then his expression closed as he flipped the page and continued reading. His chin lifted. "What am I looking at here?"

"Exactly what you think. It's the deed to Chrissy's house. I considered selling it, but you've been highly underpaid for several years for the amount of work you do. The place is worth about twenty million. You can keep it or sell it. It's yours to do with as you please. I'd love for you to stay. I know these last few years have been hard, but I'm going into partial retirement. Starting next week, I'll only be seeing a handful of patients plus emergency calls for friends. If you stay, you'll be down to two to four hours of work three days a week—possibly less—for the same salary."

Kye dropped his gaze to the paperwork again. He blinked rapidly, as if fighting tears. "I don't understand. This is your sister's home. Why would you just give it to me?"

Seth took a breath. They should have had this conversation much sooner. "Because you're my friend and I never meant to take advantage of that. My only excuse is that you're more like family to me than a friend. I forgot for a minute you don't have to love me through my bullshit life decisions."

Kye sniffed. "For the record, family doesn't have to love you through bullshit life decisions either."

That was true. "Fair enough."

. . .

Kye tried handing back the deed. "I'll stay, but I can't accept Chrissy's house. That's too much."

Seth refused to take back the deed. "It's too late. Baker already took care of everything. The house has been transferred to you, and I made sure the taxes and everything were up to date. All you have to do is throw it on the market or move in. Either way, Baker said he would help. Free of charge, of course."

Kye sniffed. He didn't meet Seth's stare. "You should marry that guy. No one else will give you as many chances as he has. He deserves to have you do him right."

Seth nodded along. "Absolutely. I'm fully self-aware this time around. He won't regret me."

Kye eyed him as if looking for any hint of truth behind his claim. Finally, a slow smile spread across his lips. "You are absolutely insane. You know that, right? You gave me a whole fucking house."

. . .

Seth shrugged. "Yeah, well. I love you. You mean more to me than a house. I don't want you to leave."

Kye looked away, blinking again. "Yeah, well. I guess I love you too."

Seth couldn't help but smile at Kye's bitchy tone. He had meant what he said. Seth loved Kye, attitude and all. He couldn't lose him. "Could I have a hug?"

Kye set the deed aside and held his arms open for Seth.

Seth's heart warmed as they embraced. For once, he felt right. His entire life, he had always felt slightly dissatisfied. Between Kye's forgiveness and Baker's agreement to stay, Seth saw his life getting brighter for the first time in a long time.

. . .

"Does this mean you're staying?"

At Baker's voice behind them, Seth quickly backed away before Baker got the wrong idea. But when he turned Baker's way, he found Baker smiling without a hint of jealousy marring his features.

Kye swiped at his eyes. "Yes, and I feel like this is somehow your fault. I don't know what you did to Seth, but I like it. He's better with you."

Seth nodded, needing Baker to know he felt the same. "In fact, Kye was just suggesting I marry you before you get away."

Baker's eyes flashed with humor. "Was he?"

Seth couldn't stop smiling. He was in love. It was crazy, since he had never believed in romantic love. Yet here he was. "He was, and I think he's right."

. . .

A sexy and soft laugh rumbled from Baker. "Is that a proposal?"

"It's better than a post-sex proposal that you can't tell your kids about someday?"

Everyone looked Aric's way as he appeared from nowhere, holding a paper tray of coffee for everyone.

When all eyes landed on Aric, he shrugged. "I mean, I wouldn't have it any other way, but it's not really the proposal that matters anyhow."

"He's right," Seth said, getting into the idea of having Baker tied to him for life. "It's the answer that matters most."

"I would say it's the ring, which I doubt you have," Kye said behind him.

. . .

Seth rubbed the back of neck. The pressure built.

Baker laughed. "I'd say it's the intent behind the proposal. As long as it's genuine and not forced or rushed because of some false sense of urgency."

Seth didn't hesitate. He knew his heart and what he needed to do. Seth closed the distance between them and dropped to one knee. "I don't have a ring yet and you probably deserved to hear that I love you before this moment, but—"

"Yes," Baker said before Seth could ask, confusing Seth because Seth over-thought everything.

"Yes, I should've told you I love you? Or yes, you'll marry me?"

Baker looked thoughtful for a second, sending Seth's stress through the roof. "Yes, to both, actually."

. . .

"Awwww," Aric cooed as Seth shot to his feet.

Seth claimed Baker's mouth. He didn't care they had an audience. If Baker married him, Aric would always be around. Between that and Kye staying, they would likely get lots of shows like this one. Not only was Seth completely in love with Baker, but Baker was also the only person who made Seth burn nonstop. They definitely had a special spark.

"Okay, guys. You two are too sweet, but—seriously— get out of my office with that. Aric has to tell me all about his dirty night with his sexy husband, and I have to gush about my upcoming date."

Baker pulled away so fast, Seth almost fell over. "Seriously? Cuddly bear asked you out finally?"

At Baker's obvious interest, Kye fell into a breathless and excited recant of his encounter with the delivery guy. Seth barely heard a word. He was too busy pulling Baker against him and kissing his cheek and neck. Seth couldn't believe he had asked Baker to marry him. He was even more shocked Baker had said yes. It would likely be several months before any vows were exchanged, but Seth was blown away by his fortune. He would make Baker proud. They would be happy.

By the time Seth led Baker away from Kye's office, Baker was barely suppressing his anxiety. He was off-the-charts happy, but that was also the source of his unease. Good things didn't happen to him. It just seemed too unreal for Seth to love him and want to marry him. The change was too big. In a few short weeks, they had gone from avoiding calling each other to getting married. Crazy things like that weren't part of Baker's life. He was stoic. Steady. Baker was not the impulsive type. This seemed too unreal to be his life. Baker didn't trust it. They had planned to go to Baker's today to grab more of his things, making this more permanent by the second.

"You're being awful quiet."

. . .

"I'm processing."

At Baker's confession, Seth pulled him to a stop. He looked too serious for Baker's liking. "I shouldn't have put you on the spot like that. If you want to say no, I'll understand. Or if you want a long engagement, I'm okay with whatever you need."

Baker closed the distance between them and snagged Seth's waist. "It's not that at all. Good things don't happen to me and you're the best. That's the only frightening thing on my end. I've lost a lot over the years. This one time, I can't." Baker shrugged, losing the ability to articulate his raging thoughts.

Seth cupped Baker's face. "Tell me what you need to feel more secure."

Baker shrugged. "I think you'll just have to let me flounder through it. It's likely I won't believe all this is happening until we're really married, and everything is settled. That means time. Do you think you can handle me being a little neurotic for a while?"

Seth's gaze moved over Baker's features. "Do you love me?"

It hit Baker. Seth had confessed to loving him, but Baker hadn't returned his words. "I love you very much."

A smile exploded across Seth's face. "Then I can handle anything. Bring it on."

Seth's lips touched his, as if sealing the deal, and reality slammed into Baker. This was real. They were getting married. This was happening.

"Yay," Baker whispered against Seth's lips in a quiet cheer.

. . .

Seth's lips shaped into a smile against Baker's. "I love you so much."

Happiness rushed over Baker. Things were fresh and would likely move slow from this point on, but Baker had found his place. He would never look back again.

TEN

WITH HIS FACE pressed against Seth's chest, Baker fought not to moan his name. Baker flattened his palms against the mattress and pushed. He stared down the line of his body, watching as his cock buried inside Seth. Baker loved the visual reminder of the sexy body he owned now. He had never dreamed he would be here.

Baker watched his glistening cock saw in and out of Seth. Aggravation clawed at his brain even as the pressure built, and his balls drew up tight. Baker buried his face again. He wanted so badly to scream Seth's name. A cry gathered in Baker's throat. Seth gasped. The sounded assaulted Baker's ears as cum

CHARITY PARKERSON

filled the space between them. Baker bit Seth's chest to stop himself from crying out as he pumped Seth's ass full of cum.

A sexy and tired-sounding chuckle brushed Baker's ear. "Fuck. These goddamn thin walls."

Baker collapsed, laughing. "Never again. The next time we invite our friends to vacation with us, we're staying somewhere else. Jesus. This trying to be quiet on our honeymoon is some horse shit."

"Don't be quiet on our account," Aric said through the paper-thin walls. "We can sleep with our earbuds in."

Seth's laughter doubled. His body shook as he gathered Baker in his sweaty embrace. "Personally, I wouldn't have things any other way. Watching you fight not to scream my name is one of the sexiest things I've ever seen."

· · ·

"We're putting our earbuds in now. Feel free to act as if we're not here."

Seth shook harder against Baker while Baker fought a wave of mortification. "Just think," Seth said against his ear between bouts of uncontrollable laughter. "Your brother could've taken the room next to ours."

"Jesus." Baker couldn't even fathom his honeymoon with his brother in the room next door. It was bad enough with Aric and Enzo next door. "Tomorrow, we're finding a different place to stay." He eyed Seth's nude form. "If only you weren't so damn delectable. Now I'll never be able to meet Aric's gaze again."

Seth smoothed a hand down Baker's body and cupped his semi-erect cock. "This is our wedding night. I don't care if it had been the Pope staying next door. Nothing was stopping me from consummating this marriage. You're mine now."

. . .

The way Seth growled the words against Baker's skin made chill bumps skirt down his body. They had waited barely a month to marry. Seth had been impatient as hell. Secretly, Baker had been too. He honestly hadn't believed this day would come. Now that he finally had the man that he wanted more than life, he didn't give a fuck who knew they celebrated their wedding night exactly how they wanted. He would still be quiet, though.

Seth licked the shell of his ear. "Have you had enough of me yet, Mr. Black?"

"Never." The breathlessness of his claim couldn't be missed. He would never get tired of being called Mr. Black.

A sexy low hum vibrated against his ear. "Good. You should hold me then."

Baker pulled Seth closer. "You don't even have to ask."

. . .

Before Seth settled down in his arms, he stole a kiss. Baker thought he would explode from the happiness. More often than he liked, Baker thought about the weeks he had pined for Seth. It was as if his heart or soul had known he had brushed his destiny and known he wouldn't be whole without Seth again.

"I love you more than anything," Baker whispered into the dark. Even he heard the way his voice broke.

Seth quickly shifted positions so he could claim Baker's mouth, as if desperation overcame him. "God. You have no idea."

Tears filled Baker's eyes as their lips met. He couldn't explain it, but Baker knew this was meant to be. Baker hadn't truly believed in soul mates and all that before Seth. There was something different about them, though. Something powerful. Baker felt like he would have married Seth on day one just to get more time with him, if he had been allowed to do so. That was how insanely deep he felt for Seth. They would be happy. No amount of time would ever be enough.

Keep an eye out for the next Candied Crush, *Beautifully Crushed*.

Please consider leaving a review at the retailer where you purchased this book. Reviews really help with a book's visibility, which allows me to continue writing more stories. Thank you, Charity.

ABOUT THE AUTHOR

Charity Parkerson is an award-winning and multi-published author with several companies. Born with no filter from her brain to her mouth, she decided to take this odd quirk and insert it in her characters.

*Eight-time Readers' Favorite Award Winner
    *2015 Passionate Plume Award Finalist
    *2013 Reviewers' Choice Award Winner
    *2012 ARRA Finalist for Favorite Paranormal Romance
    *Five-time winner of The Mistress of the Darkpath

Connect with her online:

—Sign up for my newsletter: https://sendfox.com/charityparkerson
    —Join my readers' group on Facebook: http://bit.ly/CharitysTribe
    —Website: charityparkerson.com

—Facebook: facebook.com/authorCharityParkerson

facebook.com/TheMenofSin

—Twitter: twitter.com/CharityParkerso

—Instagram: Instagram.com/sinnerauthor

—Bookbub: https://www.bookbub.com/authors/charity-parkerson

—Amazon page: author.to/CharityParkerson

—TikTok: http://www.tiktok.com/@charityparkerson